Take no prisoners!

 S0-BZO-542

General Hatvan caught sight of Rizka. "You? What the devil are you doing here? Off! Quick march, hup, hup!"

"Yessir, General, sir." Rizka lifted a hand to her hat brim in a crisp salute. "I didn't mean to intrude. I couldn't help myself. I had to stay and listen, hanging on every word. A mind like yours at work—if you'll allow me to say so, it's magnetic."

"Eh?" Hatvan expanded his chest. "What's that? Magnetic? Come to think of it, yes, I daresay it is."

"Unique, too. Nothing like it," Rizka said. "I'd have to call it downright startling."

Hatvan sniffed and preened a little. He cocked an eye at Rizka. "Recognize that, do you? Well, well, you might be a touch more intelligent than I thought."

"No, I'm just an ignorant girl," Rizka protested. "But, in your case, I can see so much brainpower lying around not being used. If you wanted, you could be twice, three times as brilliant. But it's not my place to make suggestions."

"Alexander has a flair for finding the comedic in his pageant of characters, while his chain of absurdities reveals a truth or two about the human condition along the way."
—*Kirkus Reviews*

"Master storyteller Alexander has another winner. . . . Rizka is cut from the same cloth as the bright and brassy Mickle from the *Westmark* trilogy and the plucky star of the five titles in the *Vesper Holly* series. Fans will be delighted."
—*School Library Journal*

BOOKS BY LLOYD ALEXANDER

The Prydain Chronicles
The Book of Three
The Black Cauldron
The Castle of Llyr
Taran Wanderer
The High King
The Foundling

The Westmark Trilogy
Westmark
The Kestrel
The Beggar Queen

The Vesper Holly Adventures
The Illyrian Adventure
The El Dorado Adventure
The Drackenberg Adventure
The Jedera Adventure
The Philadelphia Adventure

Other Books for Young People

The Arkadians
The Cat Who Wished to Be a Man
The First Two Lives of Lukas-Kasha
Gypsy Rizka
The Iron Ring
The Marvelous Misadventures of Sebastian
The Remarkable Journey of Prince Jen
Time Cat
The Town Cats and Other Tales
The Wizard in the Tree

GYPSY RIZKA

LLOYD ALEXANDER

PUFFIN BOOKS

PUFFIN BOOKS

Published by the Penguin Group

Penguin Putnam Books for Young Readers,

345 Hudson Street, New York, New York 10014, U.S.A.

Penguin Books Ltd, 27 Wrights Lane, London W8 5TZ, England

Penguin Books Australia Ltd, Ringwood, Victoria, Australia

Penguin Books Canada Ltd, 10 Alcorn Avenue, Toronto, Ontario, Canada M4V 3B2

Penguin Books (N.Z.) Ltd, 182-190 Wairau Road, Auckland 10, New Zealand

Penguin Books Ltd, Registered Offices: Harmondsworth, Middlesex, England

First published in the United States of America by Dutton Children's Books,
a division of Penguin Putnam Books for Young Readers, 1999
Published by Puffin Books,
a division of Penguin Putnam Books for Young Readers, 2000

1 3 5 7 9 10 8 6 4 2

Copyright © Lloyd Alexander, 1999
All rights reserved

THE LIBRARY OF CONGRESS HAS CATALOGED THE DUTTON EDITION AS FOLLOWS:

Gypsy Rizka/by Lloyd Alexander.—1st ed.

p. cm.

Summary: Living alone in her wagon on the outskirts of a small town
while waiting for her father's return, Rizka, a Gypsy and a trickster,
exposes the ridiculous foibles of some of the townspeople.

ISBN 0-525-46121-3 (hc)

[1. Gypsies—Fiction. 2. Fantasy.] I. Title.

PZ7.A3774Gy 1999 [Fic]—dc21 98-41399 CIP AC

Puffin Books ISBN 0-14-130980-6

Printed in the United States of America

Except in the United States of America, this book is sold subject to the condition that
it shall not, by way of trade or otherwise, be lent, re-sold, hired out, or otherwise
circulated without the publisher's prior consent in any form of binding or cover
other than that in which it is published and without a similar condition
including this condition being imposed on the subsequent purchaser.

For those who do not take
themselves too seriously—
and for those who do

Contents

GYPSY RIZKA

1

A Blot on the Fair Name of Greater Dunitsa

GREATER DUNITSA was world-famous—or would have been if the world had known about it. In any case, by the unanimous judgment of Mayor Pumpa, the town council, and all concerned, it was the finest place that anyone could possibly imagine.

Greater Dunitsa boasted a spacious public square with an excellent horse trough in the middle. The town clock, which frequently told the right time, was much admired. For the comfort of travelers, Mr. Farkas provided a luxurious inn: the only one, but who needed another? The town barber, Mr. Pugash, had invented his own amazingly aromatic hair oil. The highly educated Mr. Mellish taught the young folk and occasionally strummed the zither. Big Franko, the blacksmith, could straighten a horseshoe with his bare hands. Not to be overlooked: all the rest of the town's diligent, public-spirited citizens.

The only blot on the town's reputation was the girl Rizka.

She was skinny as a smoked herring; long-shanked, bright-eyed, with cheekbones sharp enough to whittle a stick. She had nothing, but was generous with it. She preferred laughing to crying; she could whistle every birdsong, and the birds whistled back at her. She lived by her wits and, since they were very quick wits, she lived not too badly.

Her constant companion was a big mustard-colored cat with an impudent tail, whiskers that looked a yard long, and a head the size of a cabbage. His name was Petzel, and he was always at her side except when he had urgent engagements elsewhere.

One early morning, she and Petzel were sitting on a barrel in a corner of the inn yard (the cook sometimes slipped them a sack of leftovers). A traveler named Deetle was hopping up and down, cursing the innkeeper, shouting for the stable boy to bring his horse, and scratching himself everywhere with all the fingers of both hands.

Rizka observed this activity a little while, then slid off the barrel and strolled over.

"Pardon me, sir, for mentioning it"—Rizka could be polite when it suited her—"but you seem distressed. Can I help you?"

Deetle left off scratching and blinked at her. Rizka wore

her usual costume: a pair of homeless breeches she had res-
cued; boots cracked and split, hardly a memory of their for-
mer selves; an old army coat so outnumbered by patches the
original garment had surrendered; her black hair tied with a
string, a felt hat cocked on top.

A reasonable person might have questioned what help she
could provide, but even Deetle's loving grannie considered
him a little bit of a fool. Further, he was in no frame of mind
for clear thinking.

"You want to see distressed?" Deetle shook a fist. "Hah!
Just let me lay hands on that innkeeper."

"I'll go rouse Farkas." Rizka was always happy to oblige
when she sniffed a chance to stir things up. "He sleeps late."

"More than I did," retorted Deetle. "Never a wink!"

"You weren't comfortable?" said Rizka. "I'm surprised to
hear that. Farkas airs the bedding every six months whether it
needs airing or not."

"Fleas!" Deetle burst out. "Fleas! They've been chewing at
me all night."

"Odd," said Rizka. "They don't take a liking to everyone.
They must be fond of you."

"Devoted to me! I can't get rid of them."

"You still have them?" Rizka set her hands on her hips and
looked sharply at Deetle. "I'd better fetch the constable. I'm
sorry, I'm afraid you're in for it now. We have laws here, you
know. A first-degree crime—"

"What crime? What crime?" Deetle blurted. Everyone has

an uneasy conscience, travelers especially, and he twitched nervously; all the more as Petzel padded up to eye him with the righteous satisfaction of a judge who has already decided on the guilt of some wretched prisoner.

"Do you think Farkas will stand by and let a stranger kidnap the town fleas?" Rizka winked at him. "I see what you're up to. Hold them for ransom—"

"What the devil are you talking about? Who kidnaps fleas?"

"You, clearly." Rizka reached out and deftly pinched a flea from Deetle's neckerchief. She held the creature between thumb and forefinger.

"Look, have you ever met any bigger? And I'd guess he's the smallest of the lot."

"Large." Deetle squinted. "I'll say that much."

"Enormous. *Pulex monstrosa dunitsa*, as Schoolmaster Mellish would say. See how he shines? That's the glow of health. Strength? You wouldn't believe! Oh, yes, they're natural curiosities, the finest fleas in the world, nothing like them anywhere else.

"Geniuses, compared with your common sort," Rizka went on. "Do you realize the size of their brains? In flea terms, that is. A clever, enterprising fellow would know what to do."

"He would?" Deetle looked blank.

"Yes, if he wanted to make a fortune," Rizka said. "He'd dress them up in little waistcoats and breeches, teach them to turn somersaults, dance on tightropes, swing from trapezes— a whole circus. He'd soon be rolling in money.

"I've heard it's been done with fleas not half as bright as these." Rizka shrugged. "Sorry. I'll wake up Farkas and find the constable. Not that I want to, you understand. It's my civic duty."

"Don't be so hasty." Deetle, carried away by Rizka's words, had begun envisioning posters, placards, broadsheets, announcements of *Deetle's Traveling Fleas*, and a river of gold pouring into his cash box. "Hand it over."

Rizka shook her head. "Can you imagine the trouble I'd be in if Farkas found out?"

Deetle lowered his voice and glanced around as if the innkeeper were ready to pounce on him, wrestle him to the ground, and strip him of the wealth within his grasp. "Who's to know but you and me? Say nothing. Here, I'll make it worth your while."

"Bribery? I don't know where you're from, but there's still such a thing as honesty in Greater Dunitsa." Rizka drew herself up indignantly as Deetle pressed coins into her palm. "How dare you? Oh, go ahead. You can dare a little better than that."

As he counted out more, Rizka handed the flea to Deetle, who carefully stowed the treasure in his pocket.

"Not a word, eh?" he whispered. "This is between the two of us."

Rizka had a marvelously persuasive smile. She turned it full on Deetle.

"Trust me," she said. "Now get out while you can, in case Farkas decides to take roll call."

The stable boy, meantime, had brought around the horse. Deetle clambered astride. It was all he could do to keep from hugging himself with glee and itchiness.

"If you're ever this way again," Rizka called after him as he galloped off to fame and fortune, "be sure to stop by. I could get you a few talking cockroaches."

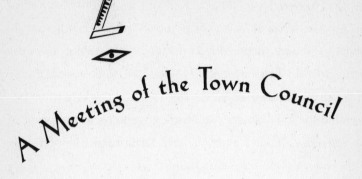

A Meeting of the Town Council

NO MATTER WHAT other business the town council had in hand, sooner or later the question came up: how to deal with Rizka?

"High time to root her out." Mr. Podskalny, the cloth merchant, usually wore a smile of contentment with the world in general and himself in particular. When the subject was Rizka, his wattles turned crimson, his eyes popped as if he had sighted a barbarian horde of moths gorging on his best wool. "She's an eyesore, a walking ragbag. She makes the town look shabby; and that's bad for business, especially the cloth trade. Pestilential Gypsy vixen!"

"Come, now, Podskalny, you go too far." Mayor Pumpa shared the merchant's opinion, but they were old enemies, and the mayor had to disagree as a matter of principle. "She's only half Gypsy."

"And all-around mutinous! Insubordinate, rebellious!" General Hatvan rapped his knuckles on the table; his mustache bristled like bayonets. He was the town's local hero, who once ventured as far as the capital, fought a war, befriended the king himself, and had come home to the pride of the citizenry. "Court-martial, hey? Drummed out of town. Quick march, one-two. Hup, hup!"

"Whatever, whatever, so long as she goes. She's a threat to public order and municipal decency." The black-robed Chief Councilor Sharpnack also served as deputy mayor, treasurer, and town prosecutor. According to some opinion, he had the personal charm of a rattrap. Nevertheless, in his spare time he was a pigeon fancier and showed surprising affection toward his rollers, fantails, and homing birds. He turned his dour glance on a little man at the end of the table:

"What is it now, Fibich? Stop waving your arms like an insane windmill."

"Gentlemen, gentlemen, please. Some aspects must be considered." Mr. Fibich was town clerk, notary, archivist, and general administrative dogsbody. The gnomelike clerk lived in a cubbyhole in the cellar of the town hall, surrounded by mountains of old documents, landslides of certificates, licenses, and forms he could never hope to complete. To console himself, he read fairy tales, which he adored.

"Ah. Yes." Fibich cleared his throat. "In regard to the drumming out of town: The town band has only one drum, currently in disrepair."

"Stop nitpicking, you wretched mole!" cried Sharpnack. "Who needs drums?"

The town clerk peered through his spectacles, indeed like an apologetic mole. "Chief Councilor, I only meant to say we can't put her out of town."

"You defend her?" exclaimed Sharpnack. "How dare you! Be silent."

Fibich, despite the chief councilor's gimlet eyes boring in on him, held his ground and persisted:

"We can't put her *out* of town, for one thing, because she doesn't live *in* town. Her wagon's beyond the municipal limits. It's true, her father was a Gypsy, but he's long gone who knows where. You've all seen the register. You know she was born here; her mother was a townswoman. So, she's a citizen. Halfway, at any rate.

"It complicates the issue, you see," Fibich continued. "Furthermore, she hasn't broken any laws."

"Then pass one she can break!" Mr. Podskalny rounded on the mayor. "Do something. Be decisive for once, Pumpa. Stop dithering." Mr. Podskalny's thumb and forefinger had begun circling toward his nostrils.

"Don't start up with me, Podskalny." Mayor Pumpa reached for the handkerchief in his sleeve.

Both men had jumped to their feet. Individuals of some

girth, they were close to bumping each other across the table. Each understood exactly what the other's gesture signified.

No one could be sure who had started this feud, but it had something to do with cheese. And rags. At any rate, Podskalny had accused Mayor Pumpa of being a cheese-faker. The mayor, in fact, had begun as a cheesemonger; Mrs. Pumpa still ran the family shop. However, Podskalny claimed that Pumpa founded his fortune by staying up all night boring holes in moldy cheese and selling it as expensive Swiss.

Mayor Pumpa answered this mortal insult by reminding Podskalny that the presently rich cloth merchant started his career trundling a pushcart and hawking fabric that melted under the first raindrop.

The two dignitaries had become such close enemies that no words need be spoken. Podskalny had only to thrust a couple of fingers into his nostrils; Mayor Pumpa knew the taunt meant "stinking cheese." Mayor Pumpa had only to wave his handkerchief; Podskalny knew it meant "shoddy rags."

"Stop it, both of you!" cried Sharpnack. "Stick to the point."

Red-faced, out of breath, Mayor Pumpa managed to calm himself. He wanted to go home for lunch. In private life, he was a doting husband and father, devoted to Mrs. Pumpa and their daughters. Esperanza, the eldest, was certifiably the town beauty. Sofiya, the twins Galatea and Galanta, and little Roswitha were blossoming nicely.

"Enough for today. I'm late." Mayor Pumpa rapped his

gavel and the meeting adjourned, as usual, with nothing decided.

Sharpnack flapped off to his pigeons. Hatvan repaired to the inn to refresh himself after a strenuous morning. Fibich groped his way down to his cubbyhole, where he took a long nap and dreamed of Ali Baba and the Forty Thieves, all forty of whom had the features of Chief Councilor Sharpnack.

Podskalny and Mayor Pumpa hurried to their respective homes. What neither parent knew, which was just as well: The cloth merchant's only son and heir, the handsome Lorins Podskalny, and the dazzling Esperanza Pumpa were secret sweethearts.

Big Franko

RIZKA KNEW about the young lovers. She had seen them rambling through the woods: Lorins Podskalny with his exuberant first mustache, the gorgeous Esperanza Pumpa resting her cheek on his shoulder, so besotted with each other they occasionally bumped into trees.

Rizka, that day, had been gathering herbs. After Pugash the barber gave up his medical practice—to the great relief of the townsfolk—a number of patients brought their ailments to her for treatment and she constantly had to replenish her store of botanicals. Glimpsing the enraptured couple, she and Petzel hung back in the shadows until they wandered away. She smiled to herself, finished collecting the herbs, and carried the basketful home to dry.

Rizka's home—the town clerk had been correct in saying she did not live in Greater Dunitsa. She and Petzel lodged on the outskirts in an old *vardo*, a Gypsy-style horse-drawn wagon. Shaped like a wooden sausage on wheels, it was snug enough inside: a few sticks of furniture, a folding table, a straw mattress. The only thing missing was the horse.

"Petzel," she said, before the cat set off on his own private errands, "don't you go blabbing this all over town." She approved of romance and enjoyed seeing it blossom. On the one hand, she had no intention of gossiping about Esperanza and her handsome suitor; on the other hand, the secret was too deliciously explosive to keep to herself.

Rizka decided to deposit it for safekeeping in a place even more secure than Mr. Podskalny's famous ironbound, double-padlocked money box.

She went to see Big Franko.

At his anvil, the blacksmith was hammering a strip of iron and singing to himself—he had a fine bass voice, which he sometimes lent to the Greater Dunitsa men's chorus, conducted by the corn merchant, who also led the town band. Big Franko stopped his vocalizing and cocked an eye at her.

"If Petzel had stolen a pot of cream, he'd have the same look on his face." Big Franko had always been quick at reading her expression. "What have you done?"

He waited as Rizka settled herself on a crate. Big Franko was not big; he was huge. The heat of the forge had scorched his face and singed his iron gray beard; sparks had scarred his shaven head; his skin was as tough as his leather apron. Not only the town smith, he was also the local horse doctor. Rizka had been with him when he helped a mare birth a foal; his hands were battered, broken-nailed, but she had seen them work with such delicacy and tenderness that it brought her close to tears—a rare condition for her.

As custodian of her secrets—he knew all of them—Big Franko would have let himself be roasted in his furnace, pounded on his anvil, and torn apart with his own tongs rather than betray her trust. She could see her latest news being locked away forever deep inside his head.

"I could have turned cartwheels in front of them," Rizka concluded after telling him her discovery. "They wouldn't have noticed. They just kept stumbling around looking silly."

"Mind who you call silly." Big Franko chuckled and put aside the band of iron. "You'll do the same, one of these days, when you go walking out with some bright young fellow. Or else you'll decide to pack up and fly off somewhere."

Rizka laughed as if Big Franko had said something foolish, which he never did. "That won't happen."

"Just wait," Big Franko said. "You're still a girl, and a scrawny one at that. When you're a young woman, you'll change your tune. And so you should. You're too much alone, you don't see anybody—"

"I see everybody."

"And friends—"

"Enough. You, best of all."

"Meantime, these years since your mother died, you've been living hand to mouth. That's a life?"

"It's mine," Rizka said, as though claiming something she had found by luck in the street.

"And you stay in that rattletrap of yours—"

"It's where my father will look for me."

"You still think so? You've waited a good while now."

"He left his watch, didn't he?" Rizka nodded as if this settled the matter. The watch was her only serious possession: gold, with a hinged lid that opened to show a miniature portrait of her mother. She kept it wrapped in a handkerchief and stored in a chest at the rear of the wagon. She had convinced herself it was a pledge, his unspoken promise to come back to her.

"When the *chiriklos* come, the *rom*—the Gypsies—always follow. He'll be with them." Rizka was at her most confident when she had nothing to be confident about. *Chiriklos*, slender black and white birds, had not been seen in Greater Dunitsa for years.

"You're a *chiriklo* yourself," Big Franko said. "Little bird, the way you've grown, he'll hardly know you."

"Of course he will. I'll know him, too. His name was Janos. I remember he was tall and handsome—"

"To their children, all fathers are tall and handsome. They're supposed to be. It's a law of some kind." Big Franko's own daughter had died at birth, his wife soon after. Rizka had once asked him about it; he had told her and had never spoken of it again, the only thing they did not discuss.

"I know he played the fiddle," Rizka said. "I remember one tune, happy and sad at the same time. Once in a while, I still hear it in my head. As if he's talking to me."

"No doubt he is," Big Franko said. "I'm sorry I never met him. Your mother—I helped her as much as I could. After she died, Sharpnack wanted to hand you over to the next passing peddler. Some others wanted to keep you."

"Some? No," corrected Rizka. "One. You."

"You'd have no part of that. You holed up in your wagon. If anyone came near, you kicked and screamed. A fighting, spitting little wildcat. When I tried to pick you up—you bit me."

"Never!" protested Rizka, knowing it was true.

"Oh, yes. I set you down pretty fast. For a couple of weeks, I left food on your step. And sat and watched from a safe distance. You sneaked out and gobbled it up in the middle of the night. Then I brought a kitten, a spiky-haired, mustard-colored creature as wild as yourself. I think the two of you finally tamed each other. As tame as you're ever likely to be. You still wouldn't leave that broken-down wagon. But I've kept an eye on you ever since."

"I'm glad," said Rizka. She winked. "Sorry I bit you."

Big Franko, during this, had been bending and twisting a leftover strip of iron. "If ever you do fly off, keep this with you. For luck."

He tossed it to Rizka, who caught it neatly in one hand. It was a bird with outspread wings. She blew him a kiss of thanks and tucked it into one of her patches. As well as holding her coat together, these patches were pockets. The towns-folk always felt uneasy about what might be going into them.

No more was said about the secret sweethearts. Big Franko went back to his work. He was making a fire basket for Schoolmaster Mellish. Devoted to scientific experiments when he was not strumming his zither, Mr. Mellish had been designing a grand hot-air balloon and required technical equipment.

Leaving the blacksmith, Rizka went on a special errand. A couple of days before, she had persuaded a flea-bitten traveler named Deetle to part with a handful of money. She decided to slip the coins under the door of the town laundress. Sharp-nack had accused the old woman of ruining his best pair of drawers and threatened a lawsuit unless she paid for them. Rizka enjoyed the thought of the laundress astonished by a mysterious gift and relished even more the vexation of Sharp-nack when he could no longer harass her.

Finishing her errand, Rizka sauntered back to the wagon in the woodland clearing. She saw nothing of Petzel.

Moments later, the big cat slid from the underbrush, in his jaws, a roasted chicken.

"That's very thoughtful of you," Rizka said, as the cat dropped his prize at her feet. "I guess you found it wandering around looking for someone to take it in. We'll have to care for it properly. What do you suggest?"

Petzel licked his chops.

"Good idea," said Rizka.

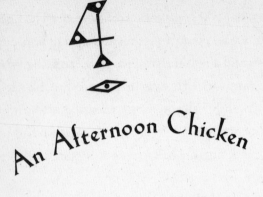

An Afternoon Chicken

THE CHICKEN belonged to Chief Councilor Sharpnack.
At the time Rizka was leaving the blacksmith, Sharpnack was
on his roof tending his pigeons in their loft. Absorbed by this
pleasant occupation, he did not hear his housekeeper announcing dinner. A few more calls roused him from his con-
centration, and he hurried downstairs.

Inhaling the delicious aroma, Sharpnack stepped into
the dining room. He found no difficulty pampering one
sort of bird while devouring another; and he enjoyed nothing so much as a golden, crisp-skinned, perfectly roasted
chicken.

He stopped in his tracks. The platter lay empty on the
table. That same instant, a big mustard-colored cat, with the

fowl between his teeth, leaped out of the open casement.

Sharpnack gave a cry of fury. He was a man of high principles, one of the highest being that what he possessed should under no circumstances be taken away from him. This included his afternoon chicken.

Robbed, outraged, and still in his shirtsleeves, Sharpnack plunged through the casement. The cat—Petzel, of course— had dashed into the street and nipped around a corner, with Sharpnack in hot pursuit of his ex-dinner.

"Stop that cat!" Sharpnack flung himself into the stream of passersby, who scattered and gaped at him as if the burden of his civic duties had finally driven him mad. Petzel streaked ahead. Sharpnack lengthened his strides, shouldering away any townsfolk in his path. He raced past the fishmonger's, past the barber shop where the inquisitive Pugash, razor and shaving basin in hand, popped out of his doorway to gawk at the disarrayed chief councilor.

Petzel darted down an alley and over a board fence. Sharpnack's last view was the cat's tail waving insultingly. Cursing between his teeth, his deprived belly growling, he halted in defeat.

The chase had led him close by the town hall. He stormed inside and shouted for the clerk. When Fibich appeared, he found Sharpnack in a sweat, pacing the council chamber.

"I want him done away with! Shot! Drowned!" Sharpnack brandished a fist. "That villain! That scoundrel!"

"Which scoundrel would that be?" inquired Fibich, who

supposed that Sharpnack was referring to one of the town dignitaries.

"The cat!" Sharpnack burst out. "The Gypsy's cat, you fool." He told the bewildered Fibich how Petzel had dared to rob him of his dinner. "You find someone to get rid of that marauding beast once and for all. I don't care how. He's a brazen thief!"

"Ah. Yes, Chief Councilor. Let me understand this clearly." Fibich began collecting his wits. Until summoned, he had been in his cubbyhole voyaging with Sinbad the Sailor. "You're making a formal accusation of theft?"

"Of course I am, idiot! Haven't you been listening? Get out of here. Do as I told you."

"Ah—Chief Councilor, I'm afraid that won't be possible."

"How not?" snapped Sharpnack. "Stop nattering and get on with it."

"Not possible now," Fibich insisted. "Once a formal accusation is made—as you just did—the legal process is set in motion; standard procedures must be followed. An official investigation, a hearing, a trial—"

"I'm talking about a cat!" roared Sharpnack.

"It's a matter of law—"

"Don't teach me law, you furtive weasel!" Sharpnack cried. "I'm the prosecutor. The law's what I say it is."

"Chief Councilor, I'm obliged to point out: As the case stands, in your official capacity you're bound by the Greater Dunitsa criminal code. I'll show you the pertinent volume if you'd care to see it. The law, as it's drawn up, specifies no difference between a human or animal offender. An oversight, carelessness in language perhaps, but there it is."

Sharpnack pondered two equally attractive choices: either to throttle the town clerk with his bare hands or to find a heavy stick and beat him on the head.

"I'll prepare the proper complaint forms," Fibich said. "They'll have to be signed and stamped, a reference number assigned. The mayor, acting as magistrate, must be notified so he can add the case to his trial dockets."

"He doesn't have any dockets, you miserable ferret!" Sharpnack paused. At first, he had been infuriated. He did not like his wishes thwarted, least of all by the town clerk. However, as he thought about it, a number of interesting possibilities started revolving in his mind.

"Listen to me, Fibich," he said. "Let's discuss this reasonably."

"I thought that's what we've been doing," said Fibich.

"As you put it, there has to be a trial. Witnesses, testimony, and all such nonsense," Sharpnack said, as Fibich nodded. "Judgment, penalty, and so on."

"That's the law, Chief Councilor."

"Of course it is. The law is sacred." Sharpnack rolled his eyes heavenward. "Justice must be done, impartially, without bias. Excellent. I shall conduct this trial, as required. I shall do my duty and vigorously prosecute the case. Pumpa will consider all aspects of the matter, fairly, objectively, and will naturally find the cat guilty. A foregone conclusion. Because the creature is a notorious ruffian and vagrant, without redeeming qualities, I shall demand the extreme penalty. The beast will be condemned.

"At that moment"—Sharpnack warmed to his plan—"I shall recommend . . ."

Here, the chief councilor pronounced a word that Fibich never before heard him utter:

". . . mercy. Yes, mercy. I shall spare the brute's life."

Fibich could not believe his ears. "Commute the sentence?"

"On one condition. The Gypsy and her beast will leave Greater Dunitsa immediately. Out of town, out of the vicinity, neither of them to set foot within leagues of here on pain of execution.

"What a useful thing the law is," Sharpnack mused. He turned an eye on the town clerk. "Don't you see the beauty of it, you dimwitted grub? Two at one stroke! If I only got rid of her cat, she'd lurk about and who knows what she'd do in revenge. This way, I'll miss my guess if she doesn't agree to anything to save the creature. If not, the sentence will be carried out, there's one nuisance gone at least, and I'll deal with her later."

Fibich shifted uncomfortably, finding all this acutely upsetting. "You'll need an arrest warrant."

Sharpnack flexed his fingers and tucked up his sleeves. "Fetch my pen."

5

The Great Trial of Petzel the Cat

RIZKA AND PETZEL had graciously welcomed their guest and invited it to attend a picnic. Petzel, with a big pussycat smile, lounged in front of the *vardo* and delicately cleaned his whiskers. Rizka leaned back against a wagon wheel and polished the wishbone. She glanced up to see Town Constable Shicker trudge into the clearing.

"You look decked out for a parade." Rizka waved a greeting to the bulky officer who had squeezed himself into his best uniform. He carried a large birdcage in one hand. "Got that rash again? Let's have a look. I'll see what I can do."

"It's not barber's itch; it's constabulary business." He shifted uncomfortably from one foot to the other. Though it was cool for early spring, he had begun sweating. "I'll need to have the perpetrator come along with me."

"The who?" said Rizka. "We don't have any perpetrators here."

"That's to be decided." The constable eyed the mortal remains of the chicken. "I'll want this bird, too. It's what we in the law enforcement profession call the 'corkus dislexus.' "

Shicker set down the cage. "Understand, it's not me. Orders is orders. So, if you won't mind, I'll just take this feline into custody."

Rizka burst out laughing. "Arrest Petzel? What have you been drinking? Go away and sleep it off."

"It's all fair and square." Shicker doffed his cap and pulled a sheet of paper from it. "An authorized warrant."

Rizka slipped the wishbone into one of her patches and climbed leisurely to her feet. She took the paper from Shicker's hands, scanned it, snorted at it, and tore it up. "There. Case closed."

Shicker made a sound like a combination groan and whimper. He rubbed his face. Things were not going as he hoped, and worse than he expected. "I wish you hadn't done that. You disrespected a legal document."

"As it deserves," said Rizka. "Anything else you wanted?"

Shicker looked mournful and unhappy. "Don't make me use justifiable force."

Rizka smiled at him. "I wouldn't if I were you. You'd have

more than barber's itch to nurse. I'll do something to you that you won't like," she added pleasantly.

"If I don't bring the cat"—the constable was almost pleading—"Sharpnack will have my skin."

"And I'll have your head. You go back and tell Sharpnack—" Rizka stopped and frowned. "No. He's got some kind of sneaky business in mind. I'll deal with that long-nosed undertaker myself. Petzel, in you go."

Shicker heaved a sigh of relief. Clutching the remains of the chicken, he hustled after Rizka as she carried Petzel to the town hall.

Sharpnack was not there. He had turned over the details to Fibich and gone home. Rizka would have sought him out, but the clerk held her back.

"Not advisable." Fibich ushered Rizka and the cat into an antechamber. "You'll make matters worse."

"I hope so. For him."

"Poor girl, I did my best for you." Fibich peered ruefully through his spectacles. "When I told him all the complications, I thought he'd give it up. But no, he's determined. He's got you trapped."

Rizka listened closely as Fibich explained the chief councilor's plan. "He won't get away with this."

"He will, he will," Fibich warned. "If you want my opinion, take Petzel; pack up and leave. This instant. Get as far away as you can. Spare yourself this trial; it will only turn out badly for you. I'll be sad to see you go, but—"

"I won't. Let Sharpnack run me out of town? No, I'm staying where I am. For one thing, I wouldn't give him the satisfaction. For another, how would my father find me if I'm
gone?"

"What else can you do?"

It was not Rizka's disposition to worry unless she absolutely had to. Now she turned unusually quiet and thoughtful, which was a couple of steps away from worry.

"Take care of Petzel," she said after a few moments. She
handed the cage to the anxious clerk. "Oh—and, Fibich,
thank you for trying to bamboozle that vulture. Clever."

"My pleasure." Fibich blushed modestly. "But—" he called
as Rizka turned away, "where are you going?"

"Looking for something."

"For what?"

Rizka grinned at him. "How will I know what I'm looking
for until I find it?"

From as far back as anyone could remember, there had never
been a trial in Greater Dunitsa. The courtroom, as a result,
presently served as a home for ruptured drainpipes, arthritic
tables, lame chairs, senile coils of rope, and heaps of odd-
ments unimaginable, unidentifiable, best left to themselves.

Sharpnack, however, ordered the room cleared out and re-
arranged by midafternoon. A high desk and a couple of chairs
had been pressed into service for Mayor Pumpa as presiding
magistrate and Fibich as recording clerk; a stool for the ac-

cused Petzel in his cage; a front bench for Mrs. Pumpa and
the girls—the mayor had decided it would be nice for his
daughters to see their daddy at work.

There was no sign of Rizka, but word had spread quickly
and spectators crowded the room, most of them standing
since chairs were in short supply. To ornament the occasion,
General Hatvan had belted on his saber. Schoolmaster Mellish, half his thoughts floating around his balloon project,
looked slightly absent. Big Franko, arms folded, stood watch-
fully in the back. Beside his parents on the far side of the
chamber, Lorins Podskalny exchanged furtively passionate
glances with the gorgeous Esperanza Pumpa. His head an explosion of freshly oiled ringlets, Pugash the barber twirled his
irresistible mustache and ogled the town seamstress, who
paid him no attention whatever.

"Get on with it, Pumpa." Sharpnack, in his role as prosecutor, wore starched white neckbands in addition to his black
robe. "Let's have this over and done with."

"Eh? Yes, yes, by all means." The mayor had been twiddling
his fingers at his youngest, little Roswitha. "Do you want to
state your case or shall I decide it now?"

"Simply put—" Sharpnack broke off as the commotion
among the spectators drowned him out. Since those present
had never attended a trial, they had no clear idea what behavior was expected and were busy gossiping. An added stir
arose when Rizka pressed her way to the front and stood
beside Petzel. Rizka's best clothes were the same as her

everyday garb, and so she wore her usual patched coat and felt hat.

"Hello, Sharpnack," she said cordially. "Don't let me interrupt. Go ahead with your speech. Then I'll have a couple of things to mention."

"You'll hold your tongue." Sharpnack glared at her as Mayor Pumpa did his best to restore order. "You're not a lawyer; you can't plead a case."

"Petzel can't speak for himself, can he?" countered Rizka.

"She has a point, Sharpnack," said Mayor Pumpa, bobbling his head at the twins, Galanta and Galatea. "Somebody should testify."

General Hatvan jumped to his feet. "Don't bandy words with her. Throw her out. Court-martial her! She's got no business here. A female at law? An ignorant girl! Disgraceful!"

"There are precedents." Mr. Mellish wrenched his thoughts from his balloon to blink benignly at the general. "Numerous examples from antiquity and the classical texts—"

"Stop waffling, Pumpa," Mr. Podskalny called out. "I'll take a hand in this and you'll see justice done."

"Silence! All of you!" Sharpnack turned to Mayor Pumpa. "We don't need testimony. The animal invaded my home and stole a chicken. There it is in a nutshell. *Prima facie*, obvious on the very face of it, open and shut. Now you can give your verdict."

Mayor Pumpa Pronounces Sentence

"OPEN AND SHUT?" Rizka raised an eyebrow. "I don't see anything shut about it. I hate to disagree with my learned colleague—"

"Don't refer to me in those terms, you Gypsy wretch," snapped Sharpnack.

"Pardon me," said Rizka. "I should have called you a temporary colleague. Now, I'll want some proof."

"Here's the circumstantive evidence." Constable Shicker produced the carcass and set it on the desk of the mayor, who eyed the remains uneasily, as if they might spring to skeletonic life.

"Get rid of this, Shicker," he muttered. "We all agree there's a chicken involved."

"It does look as if it used to be a bird." Rizka peered at the remnants like a scholar examining an ancient relic. "Whose? Yours, Sharpnack? Can you positively identify it?"

"Don't trifle with me," Sharpnack retorted. "You were discovered eating it."

"That's not true," Rizka said. "If you're going to throw around accusations, be exact. We'd finished eating it already. Besides, what makes you think Petzel took it?"

"I saw him. With my own eyes." Sharpnack stabbed a condemning finger at the cat. "I'd know that beast anywhere. He flicked vulgar insults at me with his tail."

"Yes, that would be Petzel," Rizka said.

"You admit it?" Mayor Pumpa leaned forward. "You realize you've incriminated the cat by your own words?"

"Nobody's incriminated—yet," answered Rizka. "What's to be proved: Did the chicken belong to Sharpnack in the first place?"

"Of course it did." The chief councilor's exasperation had started coming out in blotches all over his face. "My housekeeper got it from the butcher that very morning."

"We'll find out," said Rizka. "Mrs. Slatka's my first witness."

Sharpnack glowered at Rizka and said between his teeth, "You dare question my servant? Very well. Let her testify. She'll settle the matter."

As Rizka beckoned, the portly housekeeper picked her way through the spectators. Wearing her lace cap and apron, blushing, flustered at so many eyes upon her, she curtsied to everyone in sight and kept on until Rizka took her by the arm and made her stop.

"Nothing to be nervous about, dear Mrs. Slatka," Rizka said. "I only want to ask you one thing."

Mrs. Slatka dabbed her cheeks with a handkerchief and turned to Sharpnack. "What is it Your Worship wants me to say?"

The chief councilor laid a hand on his bosom. "The truth, Mrs. Slatka. The truth, simple, unadorned—"

"I was fully adorned when I went to the butcher's," the housekeeper protested.

"Just tell what you did there," said Rizka.

"Like I explained when you came to see me last night," the housekeeper said, as Fibich scribbled notes, "I went to Mr. Gulyash first thing in the morning. Before the flies got too thick, you understand." Mrs. Slatka began ticking off the items on her fingers. "I got a nice piece of flanken, a sausage, a couple of chops—"

"You treat yourself well, Chief Councilor," Mayor Pumpa remarked.

"A bit of mutton—that would be for the soup," Mrs. Slatka added. "A pair of kidneys—"

"And a chicken?" Rizka put in.

"Oh, yes indeed." Mrs. Slatka bobbed her head. "His Worship told me to be sure and get one. I picked it out myself. The plumpest and tenderest, which is how His Worship likes them. Not one of those scrawny old roosters hanging there. I don't mean to say Mr. Gulyash sells anything but finest quality."

"As we know," said Rizka. "Good. So, you did as you were ordered."

"And that's the end of this nonsense," declared Sharpnack. "Mrs. Slatka, return to your duties."

"Not yet," Rizka said to the housekeeper. "Stay here while I have a word with Gulyash."

Rizka called his name and Mr. Gulyash stepped forward. He was surprisingly lean for a butcher; a stranger might have wondered if he trusted his merchandise enough to eat it himself. Mr. Gulyash was famous in the town for his shaggy eyebrows, which seemed both to grow in the same direction; he knitted these brows, frowning, not happy at all to leave his shop closed to customers.

"This won't take long," Rizka assured him. "You agree with what Mrs. Slatka said?"

"No," retorted Gulyash. "I don't sell scrawny roosters."

"Apart from that." Rizka dipped into one of her patches and took out a slip of paper. "Do you recognize this?"

"Why wouldn't I? Didn't I give it to you after we talked? It's my copy of a sales receipt. Cash paid on the spot. I don't allow anyone credit. Least of all the chief councilor," Gulyash muttered out of the corner of his mouth. "He's not known to be quick at settling accounts."

"But I am," said Rizka. "Now, here it lists the sausage, chops, kidneys, and all?"

Gulyash impatiently tapped his foot. "I told you already. The lot."

Rizka handed the receipt to Mayor Pumpa, who ran a finger down the column. "It seems in order; the total's correctly added."

"What's the meaning of this?" cried Sharpnack. "We're not in school doing arithmetic."

"Everything's there, everything paid for," said Rizka. "Except—a chicken."

"How's that?" Mayor Pumpa scrutinized the paper backward and forward, turned it around and over again. "Why—yes, it's true. There's none itemized here. No chicken whatever."

"An oversight," snapped the chief councilor. "It makes no difference."

"All the difference," Rizka corrected. "If something isn't paid for, I'd call it: stolen."

"Good heavens, Chief Councilor," Mayor Pumpa said, alarmed, "don't tell me you're a receiver of stolen property."

"A serious criminal offense," Fibich happily put in.

"Don't blame me; I didn't steal anything!" Mrs. Slatka clapped her hands to her head, nearly fainting and tilting over backward. "Please, Your Worship, I'm no thief. It's none of it my fault."

"Of course it isn't," Rizka said, calming the distraught housekeeper. "You only did as you were ordered. You were simply acting for your employer. It's the same as if he himself did it. Right, Fibich?"—she glanced at the clerk—"as you explained it to me?"

"Dismal earthworm!" Sharpnack exploded. "How dare you explain the law!"

"And so the one responsible—" Rizka enjoyed a dramatic moment whenever it was available; she paused an instant, then raised her arm and pointed a finger. "The true, certified chicken thief stands there: the chief councilor himself."

"Libel! Slander!" roared Sharpnack.

"It's only the law," said Rizka.

"*Qui fecit per alia fecit per se*," called out Mr. Mellish, always glad to offer clarification.

"If you're going to argue a case on the basis of law"— Mayor Pumpa spread his hands—"I suppose, yes, I have to agree."

"Dolt!" explained Sharpnack. "Whose side are you on?"

"That's all beside the point now," said Mayor Pumpa. "As I study it out, I have no choice. I acquit the cat. He's free to go. Court's adjourned."

"Not yet," said Rizka, as the constable opened the cage and Petzel came out to jump on her shoulder. "There's more. If Petzel took what was stolen already, one thief can't accuse another of robbing him. So, the only injured party is: the butcher.

"He's been done out of a valuable chicken," Rizka continued. "I'm sure he'll want to claim damages against the original perpetrator. Loss of the bird itself. Loss of business while
he came to testify. Not to mention his aggravation——"

"Aggravation by the bushel," put in Gulyash.

"You might add some pain and suffering," suggested Fibich.

"That comes to quite a sum." Mayor Pumpa had been
counting on his fingers. "No way around it, Chief Councilor.
I'm afraid you'll have to pay."

"I'll take it in cash," said the butcher.

"You'll take yourself to the devil!" bawled Sharpnack.
Some of the more unruly spectators, meantime, had begun to
guffaw, flapping their arms and making chicken noises. Sharpnack glared at them, then swung around to Rizka. If he had
had a dozen fists, he would have shaken them all at her but
made do with the pair he owned. The chief councilor's face
had turned an interesting shade of purple which, in other circumstances, would have been very attractive. "Get out of this
court! Out of my sight! Don't cross my path. Don't come
anywhere near me. I wish I'd never laid eyes on you."

"Anything else you'd wish?" Rizka delved into one of her
patches. "Here, try this."

She handed him a wishbone.

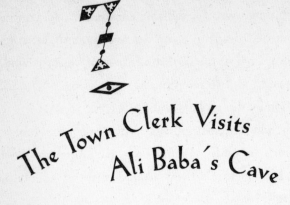

7

The Town Clerk Visits Ali Baba's Cave

CHIRIKLO, I'LL give you credit," Big Franko remarked, as he and Rizka quickly left the town hall and Petzel frisked along beside them. "You surprised me—more than you usually do. You wiggled out of a nasty piece of business."

"Did you think I wouldn't?"

"I think you were lucky." Big Franko looked at her with concern. "If it hadn't been for the butcher's receipt—"

"I'd have found some other way. It was easy. Sharpnack's such a fool."

"Yes, the worst kind: a fool with power. Things could have turned ugly for you."

Rizka smiled. "I saw you in the courtroom. Would you have let anything bad happen to me?"

"Not while I live and breathe," answered Big Franko, "which I mean to do for some while yet, a habit I recommend to you. In other words, little bird, watch your step. You haven't heard the last from Sharpnack. He'll come at you again, one way or another."

"So I'll deal with him one way or another," Rizka said lightly.

"He's made up his mind to run you off."

"And I've made up my mind he won't. No matter what, I'll stay till my father comes. All I need to do is wait."

"And keep body and soul together," Big Franko said. "And don't get yourself in trouble. Sharpnack's bad enough; Hatvan didn't look too pleased with you."

"We'll straighten things out," Rizka said cheerfully. "When I have time."

"You'll be in hot water again if you try to get back at him."

"I wouldn't dream of it," Rizka said, with a look of wounded innocence. "Schoolmaster Mellish is always telling me we should be kind to people who do mean things to us. He says it's a virtue."

"He's right," said Big Franko. "Besides, it infuriates them."

"Why not infuriate them first and be kind to them later?" Rizka said. "No, I'd never go out of my way to take revenge," she went on, as Big Franko rolled his eyes. "I just let things work themselves out in their own way. Well, all right, maybe I nudge them along here and there."

"Little bird, you're impossible."

"I try," said Rizka.

Sharpnack—he required no further nudging from her. The town urchins took charge of that. Following Petzel's trial, they capered after the chief councilor whenever they sighted him, clucking, squawking, pumping their elbows up and down. Even the youngest, who had no clear idea why they were making chicken noises at a public official, gleefully imitated their elders.

Poor Sharpnack could never put his nose outdoors without a flock of ragamuffins trailing him. His haughty pace turned into a stoop-shouldered slink as he tried to ignore them; finally, he had to halt and turn his well-known glare on them— a glare, some estimated, that could sour a pail of milk at twenty yards—and brandish his walking stick to shoo away his raucous escort. They scattered, but soon regrouped. Bedeviling Sharpnack had become an instant local tradition.

Hatvan—the town hero's comment about an ignorant girl still vexed her, but Rizka let it float for the time being. She had, at the moment, something better to do. Prompt to settle a score, she was prompter to repay a kindness.

"Fibich," she said, "you did me a good turn. I want to do the same for you."

Wondering if he misunderstood, the town clerk took off his spectacles and polished them, as if this might improve his hearing. The notion of a good turn done to him was astronomically bewildering. He made sounds resembling "Er," "Um," and "Ah," which Rizka loosely translated as meaning "How kind and thoughtful of you but there's no need; thank you just the same."

They were, this particular Sunday, in Fibich's cubbyhole— he allowed only Rizka and Petzel in the maze of old archives. While the cat rummaged through the avalanche of papers, terrorizing the resident mice, Rizka announced to the puzzled clerk:

"I'm taking you to Ali Baba's cave."

Fibich blinked at her. As well as granting visiting privileges, he had some time back confided his secret delight in fairy tales and even loaned her a book of them. He sighed wistfully. "There's no such place, not really."

"Of course there is," Rizka said, "if you want it to be. Come on, Fibich. It's not far. You'll see."

The town clerk was soon persuaded, something Rizka did expertly. He also followed her suggestion to carry a sackful of lunch to guard against danger of starvation.

With Petzel padding after them, they slipped through a back door of the empty town hall, avoiding the public square, where the townsfolk were busy at their Sunday promenade. To the admiration of onlookers, the best families of Greater Dunitsa dressed in all their finery. Half strolled a leisurely circle in one direction, the other half in the opposite, the gentlemen tipping their hats or comparing the time on their pocket watches with whatever time the town clock happened to show, the ladies curtsying, pausing to embrace and gossip as if they had been out of touch for eons.

Mayor Pumpa proudly led one procession, arm in arm with Mrs. Pumpa with little Roswitha on her hip; Sofiya, the unruly fledgling in the family nest, stuck out her tongue at the passing youngsters; the darling twins, Galanta and Galatea, toddled along like porcelain dolls in their starched petticoats; the breathtaking Esperanza Pumpa yearned for a glimpse of the dashing Lorins. Mr. Podskalny led the other procession. When their orbits coincided, the cloth merchant and the mayor turned their faces away, nevertheless glancing out of the corner of their eyes to see if Mr. Podskalny's fingers ventured insultingly close to his nose or if Mayor Pumpa was toying with his handkerchief.

Sharpnack, naturally, was prominent with his loyal brigade of chicken imitators. Hatvan, in a gold-braided uniform of his own design, accepted compliments until, perhaps fatigued by the weight of his medals, he was obliged to make a strategic withdrawal and reinforce himself on the terrace of Mr. Farkas's inn.

Leaving the local excitement behind, Rizka led Fibich into the low hills just above the town. The clerk squinted at the unaccustomed sunlight, puffed and wheezed at the unaccustomed exercise. Rizka finally stopped and pointed ahead to a gap in the hillslope, overgrown with bushes and brambles.

Fibich could not hold back a small sigh of disappointment. "This is Ali Baba's cave?"

"It will be." Rizka motioned with her head and stepped inside. Petzel darted past. Fibich, with some reluctance, followed. Rizka picked up the torch she always left leaning against the wall and struck a match to it. The chamber was shallow and low ceilinged; twisted roots hung where they had broken through the stony surfaces.

"Are there bats?" Fibich peered uneasily. "I'm not partial to them, you know. Yes, well, all very interesting. Thank you. I should be getting home."

"We haven't started yet," Rizka told him. "Go on; say Ali Baba's magic words."

Fibich had begun feeling self-conscious, not a little foolish, and expecting to be ambushed by a ferocious bat. It took a good measure of Rizka's persuasiveness before he mumbled, "Open, sesame."

"Louder, Fibich. Like you really mean it," Rizka said. "See that crack in the wall? Imagine it's going to open up in front of you."

With some added urging, Fibich took a great breath and, in a voice so strong that he startled himself, called out the magical password a few times until Rizka nodded approval:

"That's more like it. Move along, Fibich."

Although the fissure had obviously not grown wider, this was the first time the town clerk had commanded anything to do anything. To his surprise, he felt rather bold and cheerful, eager as a child to play at make-believe, and ready to stand heroically against any lurking bats. Following Rizka, he scraped through a passageway nearly as cramped as his cubby-hole. After a few paces, he stopped short.

Rizka raised the torch to show an adjoining chamber, which seemed to stretch forever into the flank of the hill. The earthen floor sparkled with flakes of mica, as if a genie had flung handfuls of diamonds over it; from the high dome of the ceiling, stone icicles glittered pink and gold in the torchlight. Petzel had hopped onto a boulder amid jagged crystal teeth taller than Fibich himself. As Rizka swung the torch around, the chamber filled with splinters of light.

"What do you say to that?" Rizka called.

Fibich had nothing to say to that. He had nothing to say at all. His bedazzlement had done something to his vocal cords; his Adam's apple bobbed up and down; he could only gulp and gawk. He had altogether forgotten about bats.

Rizka beckoned. The farther reaches of the cave were even more brilliant. The walls appeared made of mother-of-pearl encrusted with opals and moonstones. Enchanted, he could barely draw breath enough to gasp in amazement.

He did find breath enough to yelp. Stepping forward, he turned his ankle on a small chunk of stone. Rizka hurried to his side.

"Are you all right, Fibich?" She leaned the torch against one of the crystalline teeth and examined the ankle, which had begun to swell.

"Never mind, never mind, it doesn't hurt a bit," protested the clerk, grimacing and balancing on one leg. He squinted at the guilty object and picked it up. It was a shining piece of quartz. "Look at this! A diamond?"

"No," said Rizka, "but you can pretend it is."

"Can I keep it?" the clerk shyly asked.

"Of course. It's your cave as much as Ali Baba's."

Fibich pocketed the crystal and limped after Rizka, who had gone deeper into the cavern. Wonderstruck, in rapture at each gleaming rock formation, he was able to ignore his throbbing ankle—the pain had been replaced by a splitting headache when the nearsighted clerk banged his skull on an overhanging ledge.

"We'd better go back. No telling what more damage you'll do to yourself," said Rizka, as Fibich rubbed the egg-sized lump on his brow. Too caught up in his explorations, more than ever enchanted, he insisted on pressing onward.

Near one wall, wisps of steam drifted up. Fibich, whose wonderment had overpowered his aches and twinges, hobbled to observe this new miracle. As far as he could make out, it was a large, almost circular pool. A foot or so below a rim of shale, it bubbled and belched like the clerk's basin of breakfast gruel. Fascinated, he knelt and poked in a cautious finger. The mud was hot, but not uncomfortably so. Sulfurous fumes made his nose twitch. He bent closer and scooped up a handful of the substance.

Before Rizka could warn him, absorbed in his investigation, the hapless Fibich overbalanced and plopped headfirst into the gurgling mud.

Rizka was there in an instant. The clerk had vanished below the surface, all but his feet, which were kicking frantically. Rizka plunged in her arms and seized his legs, hauling with all her strength. Though she pulled him out as quickly as she could, Fibich was solidly mud-covered from head to toe, sopping, saturated with the thick coating.

"Oh, Fibich, what have you done now?" Rizka, half distressed, half exasperated, fished out his spectacles. "Did you hurt yourself again?"

"Worse." The town clerk coughed and snorted. "I lost our lunch."

"Lucky you didn't lose more than that," said Rizka. "We're leaving."

By the time they reached the mouth of the cavern, the mud had begun to dry and turn into a claylike coating.

"Fibich, I'm sorry." Rizka tried to break away the worst of the rapidly hardening shell from the clerk's nose and mouth and scraped his spectacles more or less clear. "I only wanted you to have an adventure. I didn't expect you'd twist your ankle, brain yourself—and now just look at you."

"Sorry? It was—it was—marvelous!" The town clerk's eyes lit up. "Every minute! A dream come true! I wouldn't have missed it for the world. Ali Baba's cave—yes, yes, just as I imagined. Or how I'll imagine it from now on. Wonderful—"

"Fibich"—Rizka smiled at the clerk, clay-covered and enraptured—"go home and take a bath before you turn into a statue and get planted in the middle of the square."

Rizka Offers a Course in Wisdom

AS THE TOWN clerk limped joyfully to his cubbyhole and Petzel went about his own errands, Rizka turned her mind to Hatvan. She had, following the advice of Schoolmaster Mellish, thought of a special kindness for the general: something that might help him become a better person, if not necessarily an appreciative one.

General Hatvan, of course, was not a general. Big Franko had told her the secret during one of their talks together.

"The fact is," Big Franko said, "he used to be a baker's apprentice. One night, some odd years ago, Hatvan spent a little too much time at the inn."

"He still does," said Rizka.

"Yes, but that night he was so befuddled he got himself lost on his way home and wandered down to the river. There was a freight barge tied up at the bank; he climbed aboard and went to sleep under a pile of gear—it must have struck him as a good idea at the moment.

"The barge shoved off with Hatvan still snoring away. By the time he woke up, it was too far downriver for him to walk home—which pleased him just as well; he wasn't fond of the baking trade anyway. The crew put up with him until they docked at the capital, then chucked him ashore, and he set off on his own.

"I've pieced the story together," Big Franko explained, "from travelers stopping to get their horses shod, folk who'd run into him here and there and knew the truth about the whole business. It seems he found work as a pot scrubber at a cook shop. When the owner of the shop hired on as an army provisioner, he took Hatvan with him. That's as far as his military career went."

"Do you mean he didn't fight in a war?"

"No." Big Franko shook his head. "For one good reason: There wasn't any war. A lot of bluster and saber rattling for a week or two, then it got settled and everybody went home. For another: Hatvan drove the 'goulash-cannon'—the kitchen wagon. The most frightening thing he did was ladle out the stew."

Rizka started laughing. "That's all? He made it up? A friend of the king and the rest of it?"

"Well," said Big Franko, "he did once meet a fellow whose

cousin's brother-in-law knew one of the royal coachmen. That would be friendship at a distance.

"At any rate, Hatvan finally came back here, spouting glorious deeds. He called himself 'Captain' then. The town put on a parade, voted him a pension, and handed him a certificate of municipal gratitude. Every few years he gives himself a promotion. He's been a general for a while; he's soon due to be field marshal."

"What a fraud!" Rizka, despite her annoyance with Hatvan, had to admit a measure of admiration for such brazen fakery. "What an idiot!"

"Be glad," said Big Franko. "If he had a brain, he'd be dangerous."

"Nobody in town knows what really happened?"

"Everybody knows," Big Franko said. "Word spreads, we've all known for years."

"And never said anything to him?"

"Never. Don't you say anything, either. Promise."

Rizka nodded. "All right. Why spoil things for him?"

"Not for him. For us." Big Franko shrugged. "He's no hero, but he's all the hero we've got."

The sun was just beginning to go down, though the town clock insisted on marking half past three; the promenaders had gone home. However, the terrace of the inn was crowded by the time Rizka arrived. Hatvan sat at his usual table flanked by the barber, fishmonger, and stonemason.

Rizka leaned her elbows on the terrace railing and listened with rapt attention. General Hatvan was holding forth on a favorite topic and fondest dream: a local militia splendidly armed with whatever could be rummaged from the town hall storeroom. So far, he had recruited only the barber, whose main interest centered on the possibility of wearing a uniform to impress the curiously unimpressible seamstress.

The shoemaker ventured a question. "We've got a town watch—you're commander of it—but there's been precious little to watch. Constable Shicker's in charge of disorderly conduct, stray dogs, criminal activity, and such like. What more's a militia going to do?"

"Defend the town, hey?" General Hatvan brandished his mustache. "Man the ramparts."

"We don't have ramparts," put in the fishmonger.

"We could build some," said the stonemason.

"Be ready to attack the enemy," Hatvan pressed on. "Right wheel! Load and fire! Charge! That's how we did in the old days."

"What enemies?" the shoemaker inquired. "I don't know of any."

"Find them!" exclaimed Hatvan. "Need strong measures. Take no prisoners—" The general, at this moment, caught sight of Rizka. He flung out an arm and pointed as if he had a saber at the end of it:

"You? What the devil are you doing here? Off! Quick march, hup, hup!"

"Yessir, General, sir." Rizka lifted a hand to her hat brim in a crisp salute. "I didn't mean to intrude. I couldn't help myself. I had to stay and listen, hanging on every word. A mind like yours at work—if you'll allow me to say so, it's magnetic."

"Eh?" Hatvan expanded his chest. "What's that? Magnetic? Come to think of it, yes, I daresay it is."

"Unique, too. Nothing like it," Rizka said. "I'd have to call it downright startling."

Hatvan sniffed and preened a little. He cocked an eye at Rizka. "Recognize that, do you? Well, well, you might be a touch more intelligent than I thought."

"No, I'm just an ignorant girl," Rizka protested. "But, in your case, I can see so much brainpower lying around not being used. If you wanted, you could be twice, three times as brilliant. But it's not my place to make suggestions." Rizka turned on her heel and executed a smart about-face.

"Rear march! Come back here double-quick," Hatvan commanded. "What do you mean?"

"Only that you could be so much wiser and smarter than you are."

"Not possible." The general snorted.

"Beg to disagree," said Rizka. "I know how. I have a way. Easy, perfectly simple."

"Hold on," called out the shoemaker. "You've got some sort of treatment? I wouldn't mind if you laid a bit of it on me."

"Sorry," said Rizka. "If anybody gets extra rations of wisdom, senior officers first."

"What's it cost?" demanded Hatvan. "You think you'll get some fool to pay a fortune, eh?"

"Not a penny," said Rizka. "It's a free service. My civic duty, that's how I look at it."

Hatvan chewed his lips for a couple of moments. He narrowed his eyes at Rizka. "All this blather about wiser and smarter? Rubbish! This method you have? Answer me one thing. Did you use it on yourself? I doubt it. If you had, you'd be the cleverest, richest one in town. Which you aren't." General Hatvan triumphantly slapped the table as if he had cunningly outflanked a whole brigade of Rizkas. "Got you there, missy."

"You're right," admitted Rizka. "I haven't tried it on myself."

"Well, you go do it before you try it on me. Then you'll be smart enough not to come peddling your nonsense."

"No use. It wouldn't work on me." Rizka sighed. "I'm only a girl, you see; there's not enough room in my head for any amount of wisdom. But you, General, you've got so much open space in your brain. You haven't even begun to fill it."

"Where?" Hatvan rubbed his brow. "No space here. Solid. Packed to the brim already. Out! I've heard all I want. Right turn! Dismissed!"

"At your orders." Rizka stepped away from the terrace as Hatvan went back to expounding the urgent need for a town militia and denouncing Gypsy claptrap about space in his brain.

General Hatvan Takes the Cure

THE CAT CHIRPED a greeting and rubbed his whiskers against her ankles when Rizka came back to the *vardo*. "Pet-zel," she said, "something tells me we're soon going to have a visitor."

Instead of curling up on the mattress with Petzel, Rizka sat a while polishing her father's gold watch. After some time, when she had begun thinking she had been mistaken and was ready to snuff out the candle, a volley of knocking rattled the wagon door. Petzel, startled, bushed out his fur.

"It's all right," Rizka assured the cat. "I know who it is. He took a little longer than I reckoned."

She lifted the latch and the general hurriedly stepped in. With his cockaded hat tipped over his eyes and his collar pulled up around his chin, he looked more highway robber than local hero.

Rizka cordially welcomed him, but Hatvan kept glancing around, inspecting the interior of the wagon. Finally, he hemmed and humphed and said under his breath:

"I'm not here. Understand that?"

"If you say so," answered Rizka. "But if you're not here, how can I help you?"

"Mum's the watchword." Hatvan laid a finger on his lips. "Nothing to nobody. Been thinking."

"Careful you don't overdo it," said Rizka. "You could get a hernia."

"Duty," Hatvan muttered behind his hand. "Smart, clever, shrewd, all that claptrap. Man of my rank, it's expected of me. I want my full share. I owe it to the town."

"Of course you do," Rizka agreed. "You owe it to yourself, as well. You could be smarter than Mayor Pumpa, clever enough to run the town by yourself, have your own way with it. You'd outwit everybody. Why, I can see you setting yourself up in business and making a bigger fortune than Podskalny."

"Hadn't thought of all that," said Hatvan.

"You would have," said Rizka, "if you'd been a little smarter."

"This method of yours," Hatvan said. "I'll have a go at it. The right and honorable thing to do. Be remiss if I didn't. Painful, is it?"

"You won't feel a thing."

"Have at it, then. No shilly-shallying. Hup, hup!"

"It doesn't work right away," Rizka cautioned. "In your case, it could take a while."

"Then lay on your hocus-pocus," ordered Hatvan. "Sooner begun, sooner done."

While Hatvan paced back and forth, Rizka ground some herbs with a mortar and pestle, filled a small sack with the powder, and handed it to the general.

Hatvan eyed the bag suspiciously. "What's this rot?"

"A special mixture, to begin with. Whenever you feel confused—as might happen on a rare occasion—take a good long sniff."

"That's all?" Hatvan seemed disappointed as Rizka ushered him out of the wagon. "Enough for an officer of my rank?"

"Plenty," Rizka said. "Use it only when you need to. Later, we'll see how you're getting on."

Latching the door behind him, Rizka heard General Hatvan already snuffling at his remedy.

Next day, making her usual rounds, Rizka strolled by the horse trough, where half a dozen ragamuffins were pitching pennies. They left off their game to crowd around her. They adored and revered Rizka as if she were the veritable empress of impudence and aggravation. One, a skinny lad named Bagrat, whose ears had outgrown all the rest of him, addressed his idol and heroine:

"What's up with Hatvan?" Bagrat, by common consent, held the rank of urchin-in-chief and had the honor of leading Sharpnack's chicken brigade. "He's looking for you."

"I'm sure he is," Rizka said.

"He's not in a good temper," said Bagrat.

"I'm sure he isn't," said Rizka.

Giving Bagrat and his comrades a mysterious smile, she continued across the square. Passing the window of Miss Letta the seamstress, she noticed Schoolmaster Mellish in the shop, where lengths of fabric spread over the cutting table. Rizka stepped inside to pass the time of day. Schoolmaster and seamstress sat deep in conversation, neither of them aware of her presence for a moment. Miss Letta started; she was a handsome woman, somewhat past being young, as neat and prim as her stitches; but she looked a little unraveled, a faint spot of color on her cheeks. Mr. Mellish, his long strands of hair floating around his bald dome, seemed more than usually distracted.

"My—my balloon," Mellish stammered. "Miss Letta has been kind enough, very kind indeed, to sew the bag together. Painstaking toil, it requires my continual attention—which is why you find me here. But," he added, with a sidelong glance at the seamstress, "*finis coronat opus*, the end crowns our endeavors. The result will be scientifically exceptional."

Mellish, ill at ease, shifted his bony frame on the chair. Seamstress Letta began plying her needle as fast as she could. Rizka understood this was a case where her absence would be heartily appreciated and quietly drifted out of the shop.

Halfway down the street, she heard the parade-ground voice of Hatvan:

"You there! Halt!"

The general, face crimson, came striding up. "Don't try sneaking off. Been looking for you."

He seized her arm and hustled her into an alleyway. He pulled out the bag Rizka had given him and shook it under her nose:

"Sniff this when my mind goes blank? Been doing that all day. Made no difference. Not a bit."

Rizka took the bag, examined it, then smacked herself on the forehead. "What was I thinking? General, I beg your pardon. I made a mistake. That's the trouble with being a poor witless girl. I'm so sorry. It's the wrong medicine. I gave you a cure for stupidity."

"You'll not put me off with something I don't need." Hatvan puffed out his cheeks. "Wasted my time. Now, missy, you make good on your bargain."

"Easy to correct," Rizka assured him. "Go straight to the grocer's. Buy a pound of garlic—no, better get two pounds."

"You'd have me eat all that? Vile stuff! It gives me wind."

"You don't eat it," Rizka said. "Listen to me carefully. Chop it up as fine as you can. Then rub it on your head."

"What?" burst out Hatvan. "You're mad!"

"You wanted to be smart?" Rizka shrugged. "It's up to you, do it or not. Oh," she added, while Hatvan grumbled and muttered, "make sure you rub it well into your scalp. Put some on your mustache, too, for good measure. Come back tonight; I'll see how you're doing."

Hatvan, still grumbling, turned on his heel and set off toward the grocer's.

"While you're at it," Rizka called to him, "throw in a little salt and pepper to make it work faster."

Rizka finished her rounds and, with Petzel on her lap, settled herself in the *vardo*. Soon after nightfall, a ferocious pounding nearly rattled the door off its hinges. She had barely time to open it when Hatvan flung himself inside. Petzel scurried away, coughing and sneezing.

"Got it wrong again, you fool!" Hatvan's hair was plastered to his head. The overpowering aroma of garlic filled every corner of the wagon. "Nothing! Nothing!"

"That's strange." Rizka frowned. "No result at all?"

"Oh, there's a result, right enough. Nobody comes near me," cried Hatvan. "Won't sit at the same table. Shrink away, that's what. Farkas makes me stay on the porch. If I set foot inside, he goes to fanning the air with a dishcloth. The potboy holds his nose—"

"Excellent," Rizka broke in. "A sure sign it's working. You have to understand: It's not the stink; it's the smartness coming out. Everybody can smell—sense, that is—you're getting smarter by the minute.

"They're awestruck," Rizka added. "They might be afraid how clever you'll end up. I'd guess they're a touch envious: feeling inferior, you see, with your brain going so far beyond theirs. It frightens even me."

Hatvan huffed a little less and calmed a little more. "That must be it. Yes, true. Lots of jealous, small-minded fellows running abroad in town."

"One thing left to do," ordered Rizka. "Buy a few strings of sausages and belt them around your waist. Slip half a dozen smoked herrings up your sleeves and down your breeches. And some lumps of cheese in your pockets, it couldn't hurt."

"To the devil with that!" exclaimed Hatvan. "I'll be a walking delicatessen!"

"You can't stop now," Rizka countered. "On the edge of the last step? Quit, you'll waste all the good I've done you. Oh, I should have told you before: I can only work the cure once. You won't have another chance."

Hatvan scowled, muttered to himself, and finally said, "Neither will you. I'll do it tomorrow morning."

That night, Rizka had the forethought to leave the wagon door ajar. The general, otherwise, would have knocked it down, for he burst in like a battering ram. His hat had gone absent without leave; his clothing was disarrayed; and, before Rizka could question him, he began shouting loud enough to split his lungs and Rizka's ears:

"What have you done? I've got every flea-bitten cur and mange-ridden lurcher at my heels! They take me for a picnic hamper!"

Rizka peered out the door. In the moonlight sat a ring of town dogs, wagging their tails and hopefully licking their chops.

"The last straw! No more of this!" Hatvan began tearing off his belt of sausages and pulling herrings from his sleeves and breeches. He flung lumps of cheese around the *vardo*, narrowly missing Petzel.

"Cheese and sausage? Garlic in my hair? Herring in my pants?" roared Hatvan. "To make me smart? That's nonsense!"

"You see?" Rizka clapped her hands as Hatvan stormed out of the *vardo*. "You're smarter already!"

The Barber Goes Courting

RIZKA AND PETZEL feasted for several days on sausage, herring, and cheese. Furious, Hatvan dreamed of a court-martial and firing squad; but Rizka's treatment had at least made him wise enough to say nothing rather than admit what had happened. And so he went into seclusion and spent hour after hour secretly washing his hair.

Despite his best efforts, the garlic aroma still clung like an eye-watering halo, and, finally, he was obliged to seek professional assistance from Pugash. When the ever-curious barber quizzed him on how he had come to be in such odoriferous circumstances, the general growled something about a health cure and barked at Pugash to hold his tongue.

"Ah, well, there you see the consequences. You'd have best

come to me in the first place." Pugash folded his arms and scrutinized the general with the superiority of a healthy doctor examining a horribly sick patient. Hatvan's surliness in no way dampened the barber's spirits, and holding his tongue was an order impossible for Pugash to obey. While Hatvan soaked his head in a bucket, Pugash strutted about the shop. "Therapeutical irrigation—not the sort of thing a layman can do on his own. It wants a practiced hand, sir, a practiced hand."

The barber had already performed three or four shampooing operations, all unsuccessful. Pondering the case, Pugash found his thoughts turning from his patient's stubborn hair to the charms of Seamstress Letta. The delightful creature's astonishing absence of interest baffled him. How she continued unmoved by his vigorous side whiskers and curling mustache was a mystery beyond the natural inscrutability of females. It could be shyness, or she might be dazzled into speechlessness.

He resolved to increase his efforts. So absorbed in calculating what those efforts might be, Pugash quite forgot about the general, whose head was still marinating in the bucket. Only when Hatvan impatiently surfaced, sputtering and wiping suds from his smarting eyes, did the barber tear himself from his reveries.

"Not enough?" Pugash questioned. "Heroic measures are required."

Pugash went to his cabinet, chose a razor, and began stropping it on a leather belt.

"What's this, what's this, hey?" Hatvan jumped to his feet as the barber approached, flourishing the blade.

"Eliminate the hair, eliminate the problem." Pugash tested the razor on his thumb.

"Shave me bald?" Hatvan tore the bib from his neck. "The devil you will!"

Pugash was used to dealing with reluctant clients. He strode ahead with the intention of calming the general by clamping an arm about his neck. Hatvan, with a military man's skill at evasion, dodged behind the barber's chair, stumbled against the shelf to upset a bowl of talcum powder, and retreated into the cloud of dust. Pugash, undaunted, pressed on, and the two skirmished around the chair until Hatvan threatened to discharge him from the militia whenever it came into being.

Having lost the engagement, but not his determination, Pugash chose another course of treatment. What could not be deodorized could be overwhelmed, and he set about sousing Hatvan's head with his famous aromatic oil—Élégance de Pugash—and pressed a few more bottles on the now-fragrant general for continued home application.

"If your scalp peels or blisters, pay no attention," Pugash reassured him. "It's the follicles being stimulated. The concatenation of essences takes them by surprise, as it were, and fires them up. They'll be all the better for it."

When Hatvan, with an armload of Élégance de Pugash, left

the shop, Pugash popped out of the door and scanned the street. Sighting no clients on the way to clamor for his services, he hurried into his back room.

While perfuming the general, Pugash had decided that an unexpected visit to the seamstress—who was no doubt languishing in hope of such an event—would launch a more aggressive courtship. At his laboratory table, aided by a looking glass, Pugash daubed the curling lovelocks on his brow with *Noir de Pugash*—his secret formula including boot blacking and chimney soot—and, cheerfully whistling, waited for it to dry.

Pugash did not much regret withdrawing from medical practice, though he had been forcefully encouraged to give it up. It was a thankless profession. His clients continually grumbled that he often pulled out several teeth before he got the right one, and there had been some unpleasant incidents involving leeches; but it was, finally, Chief Councilor Sharpnack who ended his career in the healing arts.

Sharpnack, one winter's night, had taken to his bed with chills and fever. The suffering chief councilor was hacking and sneezing so alarmingly that his despairing housekeeper, Mrs. Slatka, fetched the barber. Pugash poked and prodded him; inspected his tongue; counted his pulse; and, after deep thought, pronounced his diagnosis: rhinovascularity. The barber prescribed a draught of barley water and a mustard liniment to cure the congestion. Taking the ingredients from his medical box, he briskly stirred up the solution to rub on Sharpnack's chest and decanted the barley water for him to drink.

Pugash was delighted at this opportunity to serve the chief councilor. He well imagined a grateful Sharpnack, restored to health and strength, rewarding him with a handsome fee and perhaps even inviting him to take a seat on the town council; and from that position, he could rise to become—why not?—Mayor Pugash. Enthralled by his speculations, Pugash handed the chief councilor the wrong beaker.

Instead of barley water, Sharpnack downed the liniment in one gulp.

The effect was miraculous. Until then, Sharpnack's eyes had been drooping. Now they popped wide open. Sharpnack clutched his throat and made noises that Pugash assumed to be expressions of thanks. Formerly listless, he sprang bolt upright from his sickbed. In a sudden burst of energy regained, he smacked the bewildered Pugash about the head and ears, and it was all the barber could do to flee the chamber.

Still in his nightshirt and nightcap, Sharpnack pursued him into the slushy street, hurling bottles from the barber's abandoned medical chest.

Next day, Sharpnack summoned him and made a solemn promise: If Pugash ever again practiced medicine, he personally would cram the barber's embrocations, tonics, purges, emetics, and the whole colony of leeches down the barber's gullet.

Under those conditions, Pugash lost interest in the doctoring profession, but, spirits undimmed, turned happily to another. He set about concocting a range of products: mustache wax, pomade, cologne water, perfumes, hair rejuvenators, and, of course, his famous *Élégance de Pugash*. With unfaltering optimism, he foresaw his trade flourishing far beyond the borders of Greater Dunitsa.

From time to time, Pugash in his enthusiasm got the labels mixed up, but he received very few complaints since he had very few customers.

His application of *Noir de Pugash* had finally dried. Lovelocks glistening, mustache in full glory, Pugash hung a sign on his door assuring his clients that his absence was only temporary and urging them to be patient until he came back; and, with springing steps, headed for the shop of Seamstress Letta.

11

The Schoolmaster in Love

THE SAME DAY the barber resolved to invigorate his courtship, Rizka set off on her own errand. Having done her best for Hatvan's brain, she turned her fond attention to hearts, in particular, those of Seamstress Letta and Schoolmaster Mellish. From the moment she had found them with their heads closer than a discussion of the schoolmaster's balloon required, she sniffed tender feelings blossoming. Rizka believed romance should be nurtured and was always eager to take a hand in doing so. Both parties, she suspected, were too shy to ask her help, which gave her all the more reason to offer it.

Rizka decided first to drop in on the seamstress. Miss Letta, after a little persuasive and sisterly chat, would surely be delighted to accept her aid.

No sooner did Rizka and Petzel enter the shop than the cat wrinkled his nose, attacked by an aroma like a gardener's nightmare. Miss Letta, waving a lace handkerchief in one hand and a yardstick in the other, seemed undecided whether to swoon or use the measuring device as a weapon.

"He invaded my premises—and left only moments ago." Miss Letta's eyes flashed and her usually well-mannered bosom ventured to heave. "I have been importuned. Advances have been made. Yes, I have definitely been advanced upon."

"Mellish?" Rizka hardly believed what she heard. "Mellish advanced?"

"Certainly not. Mr. Mellish would never dream of such behavior. He does not"—there was a wisp of regret in Miss Letta's voice— "he does not advance at all. The individual I refer to is: Mr. Pugash.

"This is not the first time he has imposed himself. His efforts have been unceasing. He refuses to observe my lack of interest. He has, previously, confined himself to ogling— his ogle is close to being a leer.

"Now he has gone beyond the bounds of propriety," the seamstress hurried on. "He pointed his mustache at me. He endeavored to sprinkle me." She gestured toward a large bottle of what Rizka understood was the source of the aroma: *Soirée de Pugash.* "He would have seized me by the waist, and who knows what more, had I not interposed my dressmaker's dummy between us."

"So you sent him packing. Good," said Rizka.

"I made it plain—as plain as possible within the limits of ladylike decorum. To no avail. He assured me he would return."

"Try kicking him," Rizka suggested. "I'll show you where."

"That would be highly undignified." The seamstress sank to a chair and laid a hand on her brow. "And yet—I might be forced to contemplate strong measures to rid myself of his attentions permanently. Mr. Pugash must understand that he has no place in my affections.

"Allow me to unburden myself, as one female to another," the seamstress continued. "I confess that my heart is given—"

"To Mellish." Rizka nodded. "Just as I thought."

"Given—but not taken. Available—but unacknowledged. I believe our sentiments are mutual. But Mr. Mellish has never spoken of them. Alas, I have long waited for him to do so. From the moment he asked my assistance with his balloon—"

"Why wait anymore?" said Rizka. "Tell him straight out."

Miss Letta paled, aghast at the suggestion. "I am a ladies' seamstress, but above all else a lady. Never would I consider such a breach of etiquette. No, it is up to Mr. Mellish. He must declare himself first."

"Knowing Mellish, that might be difficult." Rizka pondered for a few moments. "But I can deal with it. Let's start with Pugash. Simple enough, if you do what I tell you."

When Rizka explained the plan shaping in her mind for the barber, Miss Letta was reluctant and not a little shocked. Finally, as Rizka applied her persuasive abilities, the seamstress agreed—with more eagerness than Rizka expected.

"The best of it is: You don't have to explain," said Rizka. "Pugash will understand right away."

Rizka found Pugash daydreaming in his barber chair. Out of sheer mischief, Petzel sprang onto the barber's lap. Alarmed at suddenly being nose to nose with a cat whose mustache stretched wider than his own, Pugash yelled and tried to fling him away:

"Get the creature off me! Out of my tonsorial premises! You've no business here."

"Yes, I do," Rizka said, peeling the cat from the barber's fancy waistcoat. "My business is your business. All morning, my little finger's been telling me: 'Go to Pugash. Go to Pugash. He needs you. There's something you can do for him.' "

The barber, with distaste, brushed away the hairs Petzel had bestowed on him. "You? Do for me?" He snorted. "Not likely."

"My little finger's never wrong," Rizka said. "I sense strong feelings. Passions. A lady's involved."

"Passions? A lady?" The barber pricked up his ears.

Before Pugash could pull away, Rizka took his hand, peered at the palm, and traced its lines with her forefinger. "Just as I thought. Heated emotions. The lady? Who? Let me see. Here's an *L*—and an *E*. And a *T*—it looks like two of them—and I make out something like an *A*. Does that mean anything to you?"

The barber's jaw dropped. He stared at his palm, then at Rizka, trying to hide his astonishment. "Clear as day," said Pugash, who had seen no letters or anything resembling them. "I never noticed. They must have sprung up overnight."

"There's more," said Rizka. "I haven't come to the good parts. The lady? My little finger tells me you saw her not long ago."

"Ah—so I did." Pugash looked at Rizka with growing wonder. "The lady is—how shall I put it?—much taken with me. Head over heels—I use the term without immodesty. At our last encounter, she fondled my side whiskers, flung her arms around me. Or, that is, she would have done, had she followed her natural inclinations."

"That's passion, sure enough," said Rizka. "But there's some kind of difficulty, too. Am I right? Speak freely. We're both professionals here."

The barber's face fell. "Her passion for me—overpowering, of course. That's to say it will be. At the moment, it only smolders. Damped down, so to speak."

"And you want it to burst into flame," Rizka said. "You want to waken the sleeping volcano, is that it? To have it erupt in fiery clouds."

"Yes! Yes!" cried Pugash. "Fiery clouds—my own thought exactly!"

Rizka studied the barber's palm again. "That's definitely in store. The outcome? This line here, you see, signifies: harmonious results. Depending, naturally, on how you pursue your course of action."

"I'll pursue! I'll pursue!" Pugash jumped out of the barber chair. "But——what course of action?"

Rizka put her little finger in her ear and made a show of listening attentively. "I'll tell you," she said, after a moment. "By the way, do you have a mandolin? Maybe a guitar?"

Leaving Pugash to rummage through his closet, Rizka set out for the schoolmaster's house. She was fond of Mellish; he had not only instructed her privately, he had also allowed her to listen in on his lectures through an open classroom window——Rizka was disinclined to sit indoors at a cramped desk. Big Franko teased her about this. She was, said the blacksmith, the one person he knew with a degree in advanced eavesdropping. Her affection for the schoolmaster had still not inspired a plan; but she was confident one would occur to her.

Mr. Mellish was not at the schoolroom. Rizka discovered him in the courtyard behind the building. The schoolmaster, thin legs dangling, perched on an outsized wicker hamper which, Rizka guessed, he had obtained from the laundress. The fire basket that Big Franko had been forging stood nearby amid coils of rope and sacks of sand. The balloon's bag, so neatly stitched by Miss Letta, spread over the flagstones.

"Finished?" Rizka clapped her hands. "Bravo! You've done it at last!"

Mellish nodded. But, instead of accepting Rizka's applause and sharing her enthusiasm, he turned a mournful face on her. Even in happy circumstances, the schoolmaster tended to look morose when he was not looking distracted; now his hair hung lank and listless, unable to summon enough energy or interest to float around his dome; the corners of his mouth drooped to his chin. He sighed enormously:

"Done, yes, more's the pity. *Hinc illae lacrimae*—for that reason do I weep. My work is over; and, *ipso facto*, my happiness as well. I should have foreknown its ephemeral nature."

"Mellish, what are you talking about? What's wrong?"

"All this." Mr. Mellish waved a hand at the outspread balloon. "Miss Letta has admirably completed her task. Our association—which I believed had begun to take on the characteristics of a union of hearts beyond the business of hemstitching—has come to an end.

"In short"—Mr. Mellish, sunk in gloom, paid no attention to Petzel who, sharpening his claws on the basket, accidentally hooked one of them into the schoolmaster's knobby knee—"I have no further reason to visit Miss Letta."

"That's ridiculous." Rizka took the schoolmaster's arm. "You'll see her any time you want. What's the balloon have to do with it?"

"I was going to name it *The Letta*," Mellish glumly went on. "No longer. There is an obstacle, insurmountable."

The schoolmaster grew so upset he had to go and fetch his zither to calm himself. He laid the instrument on his lap and plunked a few disconsolate notes. Finally, with a woebegone glance at Rizka, he said:

"I have a rival for Miss Letta's affections. Indeed, all too true," he continued, ignoring Rizka's attempt to interrupt him. "I must face the fact. It pains me to pronounce his name: Barber Pugash."

"Are you out of your wits? Or blind as a bat?" exclaimed Rizka. "How, for heaven's sake, did you get that idea?"

"From one in the best position to know," replied Mellish. "Mr. Pugash himself. Yesterday, when I sought his tonsorial services, he kept babbling and driveling about one thing or another, as he always does.

"He turned to the topic of his courtship. Of Miss Letta! Cad! Bounder! To speak a lady's name in a barber shop! Worse, he boasted of her passion for him, their two hearts beating as one.

"I could bear no more. Lathered though I was, I departed his premises immediately." Mellish fingered several nicks on his chin, where Pugash had tried to complete his work despite the schoolmaster's hasty exit.

"Needless to say," Mellish declared, "I shall no longer patronize him. I shall cut my own hair and shave myself. Or, if need be, I shall grow a beard."

The Rivals

I CANNOT TOLERATE the sight of him." Mr. Mellish nearly let the zither slide off his lap. "Were he to cross my path, I could not restrain myself from giving him a severe drubbing. Oh, let me get my hands on his neck!"

"A decent human being goes around throttling barbers?" said Rizka. "Is that what you taught me?"

"You are quite right. Such behavior is beyond acceptable moral principles. Thank you for reminding me." The schoolmaster strummed a few soothing chords. "I must not harbor ill will toward a fellow creature. Nor can I hope to prevail over such a rival, a man of the world, with style, urbanity, side whiskers—"

"Stop that nonsense," ordered Rizka. "Miss Letta wants no

part of him. I've talked to her. I know for a fact: She's yours for the asking."

"Would it were true," replied Mellish. "Why, then, has she said nothing to me?"

"Because she doesn't think it's proper and ladylike," said Rizka. "It's up to you. You have to declare yourself."

"But I have already done so," protested Mellish. "I have written letter after letter expressing my sentiments, pouring out my noblest affections."

"I don't understand. If you've told her how you feel—"

"Well, you see"—Mellish reddened and looked sheepish—"the letters—I didn't dare—I never sent them."

Rizka rocked her head in her hands. "Oh, Mellish, is there any dealing with you? You're close to impossible. All right, pull yourself together. Go to her. Speak your mind."

"In her business premises? Ask for her hand with customers walking in at every moment?"

"Then wait till she closes. She has apartments over the shop. Talk to her there."

"In a lady's private quarters, behind closed doors? After dark? Her reputation would be compromised, ruined."

"Meet her at the horse trough. The horses won't care."

"I do not disparage that splendid municipal convenience," Mellish said. "But—a horse trough? Hardly the atmosphere for intimate revelations."

"Then go on a picnic," Rizka countered.

"A picnic draws ants and similar wildlife."

"Boating on the river?"

"What if I became seasick and humiliated myself?"

"You could take her to Ali Baba's cave."

"A cave?" The schoolmaster shuddered. "Dank, dark, closed in and surrounded—"

Rizka's usual resourcefulness had almost reached its limits and her patience along with it. "Mellish, you can't tell me there's no place on earth—"

Her eyes fell on the outspread balloon. "No place on earth? What about the air? Take her flying!" Rizka snapped her fingers. "You want atmosphere? You'll have a skyful of it. What could be more romantic? Whisk her away; sweep her off her feet!"

"I'm not much in the way of whisking and sweeping," Mellish began. Nevertheless, his face brightened a little and he plucked his zither with more animation than he had so far shown. "And yet, it offers an example of boldness, an element of excitement."

"Better than side whiskers," put in Rizka.

"Scientific value, as well!" exclaimed Mellish. "An edifying, instructive experience."

"There's your answer," said Rizka. "Do it today, or you'll start thinking up a good reason not to."

"No," Mellish said. "Before I endanger a single hair on the head of that dearest lady, I myself must ascertain the safety of the aircraft. A short flight allowing me to comprehend its operation."

"Hold on a minute." Rizka had begun to grow uneasy. "You don't know how to fly it?"

"Certainly I do. In theory," said the schoolmaster. "I have studied the appropriate texts, thermal principles, done the mathematical calculations—"

"In other words, you haven't any idea what you're doing?"

"Not in the practical sense. Which is why I must conduct the first experiment. The reward, I now dare to hope, will be Miss Letta's hand."

Mellish laid aside his zither, sprang from the laundry hamper, and went to examine the bag and fire basket, striding back and forth with an air of courage more than Rizka had suspected and boldness more than she would have recommended.

"I shall do so without another moment's delay." The schoolmaster displayed uncustomary resolution. Then he hesitated. "I shall require assistance."

"If you're sure that's what you want to do," Rizka said, "I'll help you."

"Your offer is appreciated, but, alas, insufficient," said Mellish. "The strength of half a dozen men, at the very least, will be required. How to assemble such forces at short notice?" The schoolmaster's face fell. "No, I'd best put off the ascension until some future time."

"I'll get Big Franko," said Rizka.

The blacksmith, hard-muscled but softhearted when it came to Rizka, could refuse her nothing. If he had doubts or reservations, he kept them to himself; and, as soon as she came to his forge and told him what was afoot, he followed Rizka to the schoolmaster's courtyard. Mellish, energized by enthusiasm, had meanwhile set up the laundry hamper, lashed ropes onto it, and started a fire in the iron basket.

"Schoolmaster, you've built yourself quite a contraption. I'll give you credit for that." Big Franko put his hands on his hips and looked around the yard with surprise and admiration. "Now, then, assuming the thing goes up in the first place, what next? How do you steer it?"

"Ah—one doesn't," admitted Mellish, busily tying bags of sand around the rim of the hamper. "Going up or down is quite simple. To ascend, lighten the weight by dropping sand; to descend, reduce the amount of hot air in the bag. To go horizontally depends on the wind."

"So, once you're in the air," Big Franko said, "you're blown every which way?"

"Some degree of navigation is possible," said Mellish. "There are currents of air. One merely has to find the right ones. I have a splendid treatise thoroughly explaining the subject. I have not yet read it—but I intend to, as soon as I have the opportunity."

Rizka, hearing this, began having misgivings about her suggestion. Mellish, proudly pointing out the air-release valve and other mechanical details, assured her it was perfectly safe. Today the balloon would not float free; for his experimental purposes, it would be tethered at the end of a rope and go no higher than the rooftop, with himself in the laundry hamper to observe the craft's performance.

Though Big Franko had never seen a balloon in his life, he understood immediately what to do without being told. With Rizka following his instructions and the excited Mellish hopping around, the blacksmith positioned the bag; stoked the fire in the iron basket; and, little by little, the balloon inflated. Mellish had knotted one end of the mooring line to the hamper; Big Franko had anchored the other end to an iron stanchion in the yard.

The schoolmaster clambered into the hamper. Within a few moments, the balloon began to rise. Miss Letta had done better and brighter for Mr. Mellish than for any other customer, including Mrs. Podskalny. She had stitched together shining panels of brilliantly colored silk, and the craft hung like a huge blossom floating dreamily in the air.

Mellish, leaning over the edge of the laundry hamper, waved happily at Rizka and Big Franko. The balloon cleared the rooftop, the mooring rope tightened at full stretch.

"Enough. He'd better come down," said Big Franko after a little while, as the balloon began swaying in the breeze, with the hamper and its occupant swinging back and forth like a pendulum. The blacksmith gestured at Mellish and called to him to open the air-release valve. The schoolmaster made helpless motions and waved a length of string.

"What's he gone and done?" Big Franko muttered. "Yes, I see. He's broken the cord for the valve; he can't work it. All right, we'll have to haul him down."

The blacksmith, with Rizka beside him, bent his strength to the mooring line. The balloon slowly started earthward. Suddenly the line went slack; Rizka and Big Franko tumbled to the flagstones. The knot at the rim of the hamper had come undone; the tether, now useless, fell to the ground. The balloon shot into the air and soared free.

Big Franko jumped to his feet, shouting for the schoolmaster to put out the fire in the iron brazier. Mellish, by now beyond earshot, cheerily waved at him. From what Rizka could see, the schoolmaster showed no sign of terror or even much concern. On the contrary, as the balloon rose higher, his face was joyously alight.

"He'll come down sooner or later. But where? Smashed up?" Big Franko made a quick decision. "I'll have to track him from the ground and keep an eye on him."

"It's my fault. I gave him the idea," Rizka said. "I'll come with you."

"Step lively, then," ordered Big Franko. "We'll get my horse."

The balloon, meantime, had begun drifting away from town and in the direction of the skirting hills. Big Franko, heading for his smithy, glanced upward. "Now what's he doing?"

"I'm not sure," said Rizka. "It looks like he's blowing kisses."

The barber, all that same day, had been impatiently awaiting nightfall and the full moon, as Rizka had instructed him. Pugash changed his suit and neckwear several times and daubed a few coatings of *Noir de Pugash* on his hair until his mirror assured him he looked his most dashing.

Also, at Rizka's direction, he unearthed a guitar. Unplayed for some years, a couple of strings had broken, but Pugash felt confident he could very well do without them.

He had, on his own advice, gargled with soothing licorice water every hour or so. In the gathering dusk, he kept poking his head out the window, craning his neck at the sky as if his eagerness would encourage the moon to rise faster. When, in its own time, it finally did—and it was a magnificent, enormous moon that seemed to balance on the spire of the clock tower—Pugash tucked the guitar under his arm and stepped jauntily down the street.

Miss Letta's shop fronted the square, empty now but nearly bright as day; the moon's reflection shimmered in the tranquil water of the horse trough. The circling houses were dark and shuttered; most of the townsfolk had already climbed into their beds. No light showed in Miss Letta's apartments, indicating to Pugash that his arrival was unexpected and thus all the greater surprise.

Cradling the guitar, the barber cleared his throat. He had,

in younger days, been notable for the remarkably penetrating quality of his singing voice, which he now raised to the limits of his lungs and vocal cords. For his serenade, he had chosen a heart-melting air—he had forgotten some of the words but counted on inspiration to jog his memory.

Petzel, meantime, had clambered to Miss Letta's rooftop. No sooner had Pugash begun than Petzel joined in with long, tormented yowls. Throughout the town, alarmed cats screeched from alleyways and fences. The dogs added mournful howls to the barber's throbbing tenor, while Petzel lashed his tail as if conducting a chorus of yapping, yelling, and wailing from the whole feline and canine population of Greater Dunitsa.

The barber warbled on, bellowing like a bull calf. Shutters burst open; lights went on all over the square. Townsfolk in their nightcaps leaned from the windows, shook their fists, whistled through their teeth, and shouted angry protests.

Pugash first thought he was being cheered for his performance and sang all the louder. He suspected otherwise only when his audience started pelting him with old eggs, cabbages, and fish heads.

As Pugash tried to dodge the hail of vegetables, Miss Letta opened her casement and stepped onto the balcony. At sight of her, the barber ignored the missiles flying at him from all sides and launched into a second rendition of his serenade.

"Mr. Pugash, desist and begone!" cried the seamstress. "Though I regret the need for such an act, my words alone have not sufficiently expressed my disregard."

With that, Miss Letta upturned a bucketful of cold water and dampened her suitor's ardor with its contents. In a moment of inspiration, not part of Rizka's plan, Miss Letta threw down the vessel itself; with an accuracy as perfect as her stitches, it plummeted onto the barber's head and over his ears, where it stuck like a wooden helmet.

In the midst of this uproar, Big Franko, with Rizka clinging to his waist, galloped into the square. They had been tracking the airborne schoolmaster all evening up and down the countryside until the wind shifted and sent the balloon back in the direction of the town. Now, while the barber spun around struggling to separate the bucket from his head, the balloon scudded across the square, the laundry hamper lurching wildly.

"Mr. Mellish, whatever is the meaning of this?" Miss Letta gasped as the balloon whipped past her balcony. "I urge you to descend immediately!"

The schoolmaster was in no position to reply, let alone follow her suggestion. Miss Letta disappeared into her apartments. Rizka and Big Franko sprang from the horse. The balloon had begun sinking rapidly. A crosscurrent of air swept it sideways; the hamper tilted bottom up and sent its passenger skidding over the cobbles.

In her nightrobe and more distraught than any had ever

seen her to be, Miss Letta burst from her shop and sped across the square. Before Rizka and Big Franko could join her, she flung her arms around the befuddled schoolmaster and tried to haul him upright.

"Are you undamaged?" she cried. "Speak to me! For my part, I can no longer keep silent. Mr. Mellish, you have my heart."

"And you, Miss Letta," replied the schoolmaster, "you, likewise, occupy that site of all my tenderest affections." He waved a hand at the tangled wreckage. "I had hoped to demonstrate my unfaltering devotion by whisking you away; but, alas, that occasion must be some while delayed."

"Mr. Mellish," declared the seamstress, "you may whisk whenever you choose."

Rizka Goes Fishing

NEXT MORNING, Miss Letta and Mr. Mellish announced their betrothal, and Fibich duly noted it in the town register. Pugash, crestfallen, closed his barber shop and holed up in his laboratory, no more than a day or two, since it was not his nature to stay downcast longer than forty-eight hours.

True, his encounter with Miss Letta's bucket had caused the blacking to run in rivers from his head and his jacket carried reminders of the organic material flung at him. However, instead of bearing a grudge, he was actually grateful to Rizka, for the mixture of smells fired his inventiveness and he excitedly set about recapturing it in a new and bracingly pungent cologne he planned to offer as *Jardin de Pugash*. So, when he burst forth after this brooding period like a side-whiskered butterfly from its cocoon, he had recovered all his usual bounce.

As soon as she and Big Franko carted away what could be salvaged of the schoolmaster's balloon, Rizka went back to her daily rounds. Busy getting Mr. Mellish and Miss Letta straightened out, she had neglected to keep an eye on the town carpenter.

Karpath was in his lumberyard, caulking the hull of his boat. A widower for several years now, he spent all his spare time building it. The nearly finished craft, shored up by wooden billets, rose amid a conglomeration of saws, planes, and buckets of tar. The carpenter was doing a fine, painstaking piece of work, though the construction site was far from the river or any other source of water, even the horse trough.

Rizka came closer to admire the intricate carvings of dolphins, whales, and sea turtles covering the large, flat-bottomed vessel. Karpath stepped down from a board serving as a gangplank.

"Ahoy, there." Karpath was a thickset, big-knuckled man with a sprinkling of sawdust in his stubbly beard and a shock of hair like tangled seaweed caught in a hurricane. The more the boat took shape, the more nautical he became. He had developed a sailor's rolling gait; in addition to his striped apron, he wore a pair of seaman's canvas slops; and, acquired recently, a peaked cap that might have passed for a sea captain's. Rizka expected one day to find him with a parrot on his shoulder.

"Trim, eh?" said Karpath. "A nimble, seaworthy little darling—she's yare, wouldn't you say?"

"Yare? Oh, yes," agreed Rizka, "she's yare as anything I've ever seen."

Petzel, meanwhile, hopped smartly aboard as if he had been a ship's cat ever since he was a kitten. Karpath moistened a finger and held it up to gauge the wind, of which, at the moment, there was none.

"Aye, shipshape she'll be," said Karpath, "when the time comes."

"You're sure it will?"

"A flood like you wouldn't believe." Karpath bobbed his head happily. The prospect of inevitable, inescapable disaster—and the means to survive it—made him lighthearted. He could hardly wait. "Cloudbursts. Inundations. I know what I know."

Karpath had an eye and hand so practiced he could saw a plank to exact size without measuring and drive a nail home with a single hammer blow. No question of his skill, but his wits; town gossip calculated that since losing Mrs. Karpath— who never would have put up with such nonsense—he had also lost three quarters of them. The weather in Greater Dunitsa, like everything else, was the best imaginable, to the extent that it snowed only in deep winter, was unbearably hot only in summer, and rained only on cloudy days. The townsfolk tapped their heads and rolled their eyes, but never in his presence. Karpath not only had a skilled hand and eye but, as well, a strong arm.

The carpenter, in any case, shrugged off popular opinion and paid as much attention to it as he would to a weevil in a ship's biscuit, not that he had ever seen a weevil or a ship's biscuit. With the help of Fibich, he delved into the town archives, pored over weather reports from as far back as the clerk could dredge them up. Greater Dunitsa had never known a flood; the carpenter took the logical position that if something had never happened, sooner or later it would. In proof of his confidence, he was building his boat in the lumberyard. When the town was under water—he envisioned Sharpnack clinging for dear life to the clock tower—the vessel would float on its own.

"When do you reckon it's going to start?" Rizka never made fun of Karpath. As Big Franko once told her, it was wise to keep an open mind about lunatics and doomsayers; they could turn out to be right. "You'll let me know a little ahead, so I can take care of my wagon."

"Don't worry about it," said Karpath. "I'll bring you aboard and your cat, too."

Rizka thanked him for his kindness. She was about to continue on her rounds when Karpath called to her:

"If you go by the fishmonger's, you give Sobako a message: He should stuff an eel up his nose."

"Why would he want to?"

Karpath snorted. "Skinflint! Cheapskate! He asked me to paint a sign for his shop. Lubber! I asked a fair price for the work. Now, says he, it's too high. Belay all that! I've got better things to do than haggle with him. He can go boil his head in a pot of chowder. You tell him that."

"Gladly." Rizka was none too fond of Sobako since he tried to make her pay for a few fish heads he would have thrown out in the first place. Also, it occurred to her that Petzel was partial to seafood, and neither she nor the cat had eaten any since the herrings General Hatvan had flung out of his pants.

"Come on, Petzel. Let's see what we can do." By the time Rizka stepped inside Sobako's shop, the cat was already licking his chops.

The fishmonger, with a long face as hard and dry as his salted codfish, bent over a wooden board propped on his counter. Before Rizka could deliver the carpenter's suggestions, Sobako started up and cast around for something to throw at Petzel.

"Keep that creature away from my fish barrels," ordered Sobako. "Who wants goods that some cat's been sniffing at? I can't sell what's been pawed and poked. If you're here to buy, put up your money first."

"I have a message for you," Rizka said. "From Karpath. About eels—"

"I don't want to hear it. No more dealings with that madman. A robber on top of a lunatic. I ask him to paint a sign.

He means to charge me for each word. Each word, mind you! And extra for a picture of a fish. What, he takes me for a fool?" Sobako squinted one eye and laid a finger on his brow. "I'm just a little sharper than he thinks. Who outwits Sobako? I'll tell you: nobody. I'm doing the job myself."

Rizka glanced at the blank signboard. Sobako had done nothing much beyond setting out pots of paint and a few brushes. "Very attractive—so far. What are you going to put on it?"

Sobako held up a scrap of paper. "Something eyecatching to draw customers. As Mrs. Sobako always tells me, 'Sobako, you've got a way with words.' Here it is: *Fresh fish sold here daily*."

"You certainly do have a way with words," Rizka agreed.

Sobako nodded, then frowned. "It's painting the letters— there's the trouble. They come out scrawly. But I'll manage."

"You're sure?" said Rizka. "It takes practice. You're a busy fellow, with a lot on your mind. Do you have time for it? Enough that you had the idea. Let somebody else take care of the rest." She studied the scrap of paper and pursed her lips. "Sobako, I'll tell you what. I'll do it for you. Right now."

A shrewd look swam into Sobako's face and floated there a while. Then he said, "How much? Don't try cheating me, either."

"Wouldn't dream of it," said Rizka. "What about half as much as Karpath wanted? Fair enough?"

"No." Sobako privately counted on his fingers, calculating how much extra he could save. "One third the price, that's all you deserve. And you get nothing till you're finished."

"Done," said Rizka. "Better yet, I'll pare down your expense even more. Look at this"—she could see the fishmonger's interest was well hooked—"*Fresh fish sold here daily*? You don't sell them nightly, do you? Of course not. So why bother with *daily*? A word less, and less to pay."

"Eh, that's right," Sobako replied. "Get rid of it. More cost for no purpose? I'd be stupid to pay for what I don't need."

"Something else." Rizka cupped her chin in her hand. "*Fresh fish sold here.* That's good. But—why say *here*? Where else would you sell them?"

"Get rid of that, too," Sobako ordered.

Rizka picked up a brush. "Wait. Come to think of it, why bother saying *sold*? You're clearly not giving them away."

"Strike it out!" cried Sobako. "I give nothing away. Everybody knows that."

"Now, then," said Rizka, "what about *fresh*? You don't sell stale fish, do you?"

"The best. Who'd come for rotten fish?"

"We'll strike out *fresh* as well. And—who needs to say *fish*? You can smell them all over town."

"You certainly can," Sobako said proudly. "No need to write it out." He laughed in his throat. "And you. Hah! You've talked yourself out of a job and I've saved my money."

"There's still a picture of a fish to paint."

"Hum. So there is. Get to it, then."

"I'll need a model," said Rizka. "What about—yes, that handsome mackerel in the barrel. Let's have a look."

Sobako fetched out the mackerel and flopped it on the counter. Rizka studied the fish from all angles; moved it here and there; propped it one way to catch the light; then, dissatisfied, propped it the other way to catch the shadow; turned it sideways, head first, tail first; and finally threw up her hands.

"It won't do," she said. "I can't get the true fishiness of it. No use. It won't look right at all. You don't really need it anyway."

"What about my signboard?" cried Sobako.

"That's the beauty of it," Rizka said. "A sign with nothing on it that says everything. Who's seen anything like it? You'll be the talk of the town."

"Why—so I will!" Sobako exclaimed. "And never cost me a penny! Because you'll get no pay from me, I can tell you."

"That's all right; I'm glad to be helpful," Rizka said. "I'll even get rid of that old mackerel for you."

"Old? It's brand new. What are you talking about?"

"It's a secondhand mackerel now," Rizka said. "A used fish. An artist's model—that's taken all the good out of it. Look at those dull eyes. The scales—shaggy, practically falling off. You wouldn't sell merchandise like that. I'll dispose of it. Don't worry; I won't charge you."

"Get the thing out of my shop." Sobako stared in distaste. "I won't have this mess hanging around spoiling my reputation. Get yourself out of here, too."

Rizka, with Petzel trotting after her, tucked the mackerel under her arm and waved good-bye to the fishmonger. Sobako, chuckling and rubbing his hands, hurried upstairs to his living quarters. He could hardly wait to tell Mrs. Sobako how cleverly he had outwitted Rizka.

14

The Illustrious Doctor Skizzarkus

PETZEL AND RIZKA enjoyed their dinner. Chief Councilor Sharpnack did not enjoy his. Since the infamous trial, his diet had become distressingly limited. Rizka had humiliated him, made him look like a fool, turned him into a laughingstock, and ruined his taste for chicken. The mere sight of one on his platter sent him into convulsions, spasms, choking fits, and seasickness. He also recoiled in horror from duck, goose, and turkey, and even eggs, which he saw as future chickens. Mrs. Slatka, his housekeeper, finally gave up serving him fowl of any sort.

Sharpnack now spent many late hours pondering how to settle the score with Rizka: not in revenge but as a sacred duty. In his private office, he pored over volumes of statutes and regulations. Sharpnack devoutly believed that everyone, except himself, if properly scrutinized, was a criminal of some kind or other. So far, in the case of Rizka, he could winkle out nothing to prosecute.

One night, he was gloomily studying an index of local ordinances. His candle had guttered down to a stump; his eyes blurred as he squinted at the columns of fine print. Suddenly his nose twitched, his face lit up, and he blinked like a weary gold-seeker who miraculously stubs his toe on a glittering nugget the size of his head.

"Yes! That's it!" Sharpnack could barely keep from jumping up and dancing a little jig. "You Gypsy trickster, now I've got you!"

"Fibich, what's this new nonsense he's come up with?" Rizka, in her wagon, was boiling herbs while the town clerk slumped on a bench.

"It isn't nonsense. I'm telling you he's really going ahead with it." Fibich was being treated for writer's cramp, but he would have hurried to the *vardo* in any case. His devotion to Rizka had grown all the more since his glorious adventure in Ali Baba's cave. "He announced it this morning at the council meeting. I came here as soon as I could.

"There's no stopping him. I just thought you'd best know ahead of time." Fibich groaned. "He found a special regulation. A little vague, but what it means is—Ouch! Ouch!"— Rizka had applied a hot compress to the clerk's arm and elbow—"yes, well, it means whatever he wants it to mean. He's head of the Greater Dunitsa Board of Trade, Commerce, and Industry; it's his department; he can do as he pleases. What it comes down to: Nobody can practice medicine without his written permission."

"A license?" Rizka said. "Annoying, but I suppose I'll have to apply."

"He'll never give you one."

Rizka shrugged. "So I'll practice without it."

"He expects you to," Fibich said. "If you do, there's a heavy fine."

"Simple," said Rizka. "I won't pay."

"He expects that, too. But there's another part of the law: Anyone who consults an unlicensed doctor—*they* have to pay an even bigger fine. Who'll come to you if it costs them a fortune in penalties?"

"I see his game." Rizka frowned thoughtfully. "But the town won't have a doctor. Unless Pugash takes up medicine again, and that would be a disaster."

"Sharpnack doesn't care, as long as your trade's ruined. You barely make a living. Now you'll make nothing at all. Dear girl, he'll turn you into a beggar. Or drive you away. That's what he's always wanted."

"When I go, it won't be his doing. My decision. Not his." Rizka tightened her lips and set about preparing another compress. By the time she finished, she had calculated how to deal with Sharpnack.

"Can you rummage out a few things for me? I'll come get them in a little while," she said, as Fibich nodded. "And you," she told Petzel, who had been sitting on his haunches and observing the proceedings like a consulting physician, "you can do me a special favor."

Sharpnack had never been more cheerful. Except for his dietary hardship, he found the world an excellent, well-ordered place. The only thing that marred his spirits was Fibich, who ventured into his private office.

"Chief Councilor, I don't mean to disturb you—"

"Then don't." Sharpnack scowled at him.

"Yes, Chief Councilor. But there's an individual outside. A visitor quite favorably impressed by the town. He wants to present his compliments to the authorities. Mayor Pumpa's still out to lunch, so I was thinking—"

"Don't do that either. You cringing hedgehog, do you suppose I have time to waste on gawking travelers?"

"He's not a gawker, Chief Councilor. He's a distinguished personage. An illustrious doctor."

Sharpnack pricked up his ears. "Is he, indeed?"

"Yes, Chief Councilor. A genius in his profession, as he himself assured me. Personal physician to any number of crowned heads, ministers of state— His name is Dr. Skizzarkus."

"Show him in," ordered Sharpnack.

Fibich beckoned to a black-robed figure wearing an academic mortarboard on his head and, slightly askew on his nose, a pair of green-tinted spectacles. A short orangy-mustardy beard covered much of the learned doctor's face—Petzel had allowed Rizka to clip off some of his fur and paste it on her cheeks. The illustrious physician presented a rather eccentric air, which all the more convinced Sharpnack his visitor was most certainly a genius.

"Dr. Skizzarkus, I presume?" Sharpnack offered the rare courtesy of a nod. "I am honored to make your acquaintance."

"Of course you are." Rizka assumed a wheezy, raspy voice. "For my part, I wish to compliment you on your splendid town, a credit to public servants like yourself. I was much impressed by its many attractions and the excellence of your municipal horse trough among other amenities.

"I tell you in confidence, Councilor Sharkhead—ah, Sharpnose, whatever—I am seeking a tranquil place far from the city's hustle and bustle where I may set up my practice and pursue my research.

"Indeed, sir, I might well contemplate installing myself in this salubrious environment," Rizka continued. "I must first, however, inquire as to the present number of medical practitioners. I would find it beneath my dignity to compete with provincial physicians."

"My dear doctor, you arrive at the perfect moment," said Sharpnack. "I am in process of eliminating from practice a Gypsy charlatan who dares to foist her quackery on unsuspecting patients. A disgusting creature, disrespectful, insolent, an evil influence on our wholesome community. But I assure you, sir, she will be extirpated, crushed, driven out—"

So carried away by his own words, Sharpnack had to fan himself with his handkerchief. "Forgive me, sir. If you knew her you would understand my vehemence. The point is: In effect, we have no town doctor. The medical field will be yours entirely.

"I am also instituting a strict system of licensing," Sharpnack went on more calmly. "In your case, a mere formality. I assume you have all proper credentials."

"Certainly. My numerous diplomas and certificates, along with my staff of servants and assistants, as well as my extensive laboratory and diagnostic equipment, will arrive by freight barge tomorrow. Meantime, I shall give the matter careful consideration and convey to you my decision. For tonight, I shall take lodgings at your local inn."

"No, sir, you shall not," declared Sharpnack. "Mr. Farkas is famous for his accommodations, but a public house for one of your distinction? No, you shall be an honored guest in my home and stay as long as you wish. Indeed, I insist upon it."

Surprised by the unforeseen invitation, Rizka wheezed her acceptance. This turn of events was better than she had expected, and she allowed Sharpnack to conduct her from the town hall to his residence.

There, Sharpnack led his guest into the dining room and instructed Mrs. Slatka to prepare her tastiest dinner. As the housekeeper curtsied her way into the kitchen, Sharpnack drew his visitor aside:

"My dear colleague—as I consider you to be, since you cure the physical body while I cure the body politic—allow me to consult with you regarding a personal, intimate matter." Sharpnack lowered his voice to a whisper. "I have, these days, been suffering from a most disturbing affliction. I find myself unable to enjoy my favorite dish, chicken, nor even tolerate the sight of it. The effect upon me is horrendous. A curious condition."

"Not curious at all." Rizka adjusted her green spectacles and peered intently at Sharpnack. "Your ailment, as we in the profession call it, is: chickophobia complicated by pulletosis. More common than you might suppose. I myself have treated dozens of cases. It originates in a mental disturbance but leads to gravest physical consequences. Most typically, the patient's nose falls off."

"Monstrous! Horrible!" Sharpnack's face went fish-belly white. "I am lost!"

"Not to worry. After the nose falls off, another one grows in its place, in shape and texture like a chicken's beak, in some cases, a duck bill. You will be quite capable of leading a normal life, as normal as possible, that is, in such circumstances."

"Chicken beak? Duck bill?" Sharpnack, trembling, seized the physician's arm. "Dr. Skizzarkus, cure me! I implore you!"

"Gladly. The cure is quite simple. Time, however, is of the

essence. You have waited perhaps too long. By my observation, your nose could drop off within a few hours or sooner. Immediate therapy will be required if there is any chance of saving you."

"Do it!" Sharpnack clapped his hands to his nose. "Do it instantly!"

"I shall make every effort, but you must follow my instructions to the letter. Put yourself entirely in my hands. Tell me, sir, do you have an enclosure? A cage of some sort?"

Sharpnack stammered that he had an old pigeon coop in the shed; and, as ordered, ran to haul it into the courtyard, all the while gripping his nose as if it might part company with his face at any moment. Rizka, finding Mrs. Slatka in the kitchen, explained what she required. As the puzzled housekeeper sped off, Rizka took a pot of honey and a long spoon and, with solemn doctorial tread, went to join Sharpnack at the coop.

"Excellent. Now, Chief Councilor, be kind enough to disrobe. Come, sir, no false modesty. I am, after all, a physician."

By the time Mrs. Slatka returned, Sharpnack was shivering in his drawers and rubbing the gooseflesh on his skinny arms. Blushing, averting her eyes, she set down the sack she had brought from Mr. Gulyash's butcher shop: its contents, a bushel of chicken feathers.

Rizka had already spooned out the honey and applied it to Sharpnack's head, face, chest, and as much of the rest of him as her supply allowed. Now she reached into the sack.

"Dr. Skizzarkus, what cure is this?" blurted Sharpnack as Rizka plastered him with the feathers.

"You must find your inner chicken." Rizka dipped out more handfuls of feathers and sifted them onto Sharpnack. "As your condition was originally mental, you must put yourself in the proper philosophical frame of mind. Be in touch with the chicken side of your nature. Embrace it; come to know and love it. In short, become one with the Cosmological Chicken. It would help if you clucked and tried to lay an egg. Now, sir, please enter."

Too terrified to question, Sharpnack squeezed himself into the coop. Rizka bolted it securely and drew Mrs. Slatka aside:

"Confinement is essential to the success of his treatment. No matter what he says, ignore him. I shall return momentarily."

Leaving Sharpnack clucking and squawking, gripping his nose, and straining as if he actually meant to lay an egg, Rizka left the courtyard. Once out of sight, she discarded the robe and headpiece and cleaned Petzel's hair from her face. Then, in her usual garb, she strolled back.

"How dare you come here?" Sharpnack, in full plumage, shouted from behind the bars. "Serious medical procedures are taking place. Be off, you Gypsy spawn!"

"I'm only bringing you a message," Rizka said, "from— what's his name? Dr. Gazorkus? I just ran into him crossing the square. He wants you to know he's changed his mind. He decided not to stay in town. By now, he's long gone."

"My treatment!" bawled Sharpnack. "Find him! My nose depends on it!"

"Oh, that," said Rizka. "He explained everything to me. He said you were nearly cured. All you do now is run three times around the yard. Do it right away or the cure fails and you'll be worse off than before."

"Mrs. Slatka," Sharpnack ordered, "unbolt this coop."

"Your Worship, Dr. Skizzarkus told me I shouldn't." The housekeeper curtsied apologetically. "I'm to pay no mind to anything you say."

"Then you," Sharpnack yelled at Rizka, "you let me out!"

"I'd like to. Sorry I can't," said Rizka. "I'd be taking part in your treatment and that's the same as practicing medicine without a license. But—wait." Rizka paused as Sharpnack flung himself against the bars. "I see a way around it."

She reached into her pocket and took out a pen, ink bottle, and sheet of paper. "Write down your permission. On your authority, I'm officially Dr. Rizka."

"Yes, yes!" wailed Sharpnack. "Give it here. Quick!"

Rizka pushed pen and paper through the bars. Sharpnack scribbled as she directed and thrust the license into her hands. Rizka scanned it, nodded approval, and opened the coop.

"Now," she said, as Sharpnack scrambled out, "go ahead, start running. My professional advice is: Be sure to keep your knees good and high. Oh—if your nose ever comes loose, make an appointment and I'll stitch it on for you."

15

Terror in Greater Dunitsa

IN ADDITION TO practicing her own style of medicine, Rizka taught school whenever she had an hour or so to spare. She gave courses of instruction in elementary-level sciences: long-distance spitting, whistling through the fingers, standing on the head, juggling three balls, shuffling cards one-handed, and whatever else came to mind. Her class consisted of one pupil: Mayor Pumpa's daughter, Sofiya.

Absolutely forbidden to go anywhere near Rizka, Sofiya naturally spent as much time as possible with her. A couple of years younger than her teacher, Sofiya had already developed a Rizka-like swagger and longed for ragged trousers instead of skirts and starched aprons. To the dismay of her doting parents, she cocked her feet on the best furniture and picked her teeth with a broom straw. She achieved highest grades in nipping out of windows and shinnying up and down drainpipes. During the Sunday promenade, she made the most horrible faces and disgusting noises at the passing lads, which only increased their lovesick yearning. She would grow up to be a heartbreaker.

Though Rizka never asked a fee for this private tutoring, Sofiya often smuggled portions of the Pumpa dinners to her professor, leaving Mrs. Pumpa to puzzle over why the Sunday roast never stretched as far as she calculated. Sofiya adored Petzel, as well, and brought him special tidbits at the expense of the mayor's between-meal snacks.

As Rizka's prize student and apprentice demon, Sofiya enjoyed a special privilege: Rizka let her look at the gold watch and admire the little portrait inside.

"It's beautiful," Sofiya whispered. "Do you think your father's ever coming back for it?"

"Of course. That's why I'm waiting."

"And he'll take you away with him? You'll go all over the world?" Sofiya was as excited as if it were happening to herself. "But why did he leave in the first place? Didn't he love you?"

"I'll find out when he's here." Rizka wrapped the watch in the handkerchief and returned it to the chest. "I'll ask him."

Rizka, one day, was tidying up the wagon when Sofiya burst in, cheeks flushed, pigtails flying, beside herself with happy excitement and angry tears.

"In an alley—I found them! Left to die!" Sofiya undid the sack she held in her arms and spilled out the contents, or, rather, the contents spilled themselves out and scampered over the floor: five mustard-colored kittens with enormous whiskers and heads that would surely grow to the size of cabbages. Petzel expertly rounded them up, licked their ears, and calmed the mewing kittens with reassuring purrs. Sofiya, vowing revenge on the doer of such a cruel deed, carried on so indignantly that Rizka had to take her by the braids and sit her down on the floor beside Petzel.

"Be calm, little one. The important thing is: The kittens are safe," Rizka said. "They can stay here. Petzel will see to them. They're no doubt some of his relatives. He has families all over town, that rascal"—she laughed—"which is more than I can say for myself."

"Couldn't I keep them?" Sofiya pleaded. "I'm the one who found them. I always wanted a cat."

"I'm sure Petzel will be glad if they have a good home," said Rizka. "They're yours."

Sofiya looked ready to burst into tears again. "The trouble is—my father won't have a cat in the house, let alone five. I've asked him a thousand times. He waves his arms and gets red in the face. Then he shouts a lot."

"He just needs a little persuasion. Don't worry, you'll have your kittens."

Sofiya brightened immediately. "Sure? How?"

"I'm thinking." Rizka had already considered several possibilities and rejected them. As an artist in her profession, she relished a challenge, the more difficult the better. "It could be a good chance for you to learn something—beyond the ordinary whining, pouting, sulking, begging, threatening to starve yourself. They're all useful, if you put them together the right way, no style and flair, though. Your father's the mayor, so this should be grand, large-scale."

"Let's do it." Sofiya looked at Rizka with glowing admiration. "Do what?"

"I'm beginning to see how it can work." A distant gaze had come into Rizka's eyes, as if she were contemplating a vast and dazzling panorama: "For a start, I'll need a couple of things from Big Franko. You, little one, can you borrow one of your mother's nightgowns? Good. Now, you know the back door to the town hall? Meet me there, but don't let anybody see you hanging around."

"Then?"

"I'll show you," Rizka said. "Watch and learn."

The town hall was considered an architectural gem, a municipal masterpiece, the ornament of Greater Dunitsa. And so, of course, it was—from the outside. But the builder, during a fuddled, bleary-eyed morning, after a night of merrymaking, had misread his plans. Instead of meeting properly, the interior frameworks had only a nodding acquaintance with each other; flues and drains drifted a little askew; behind the plastered walls, gaps opened where none should be. Not even

Fibich knew about it; but Rizka, prowling and poking around where she had no business, discovered the structure's inner secret. She explored passages and crawlspaces, improved and enlarged them, and gave herself free run of the building's intestinal tract. Invisible, unsuspected, she could even eavesdrop on council meetings whenever she felt like it, which was not often, for they usually put her to sleep.

Rizka decided to share the secret with her prize pupil. This, she felt, was the moment to advance Sofiya's education to a higher level. After dropping in on Big Franko—the blacksmith frowned uneasily until Rizka confided what she had in mind—she met Sofiya as agreed; the two of them slipped unobserved through the back door and into the passageways.

General Hatvan, as commander of the town watch, enjoyed the privileges of rank by leading his night patrol from a table in Mr. Farkas's inn. His personal presence was not required; there was little either to watch or command. The barber's serenade and the schoolmaster's balloon provided the only disturbance in recent memory but constituted no threat to municipal security.

Toward midnight, the general had grown drowsy, leaning back in his chair, mouth ajar, eyes on their way to complete shutdown. Farkas had long gone to bed. Only Hatvan's devotion to duty and a platter of sausages kept him at his post. He surrendered, at last, to the overwhelming assault of slumber.

Next thing he knew, his lieutenant, Pugash, was grabbing him by the shoulders and yelling in his ears. The barber's face was ashen, his mustache and side whiskers in desperate condition. Before Hatvan could reprimand his second in command for laying hands on a sleeping superior officer, Pugash hauled him out of the chair and propelled him through the door.

"The clock!" bawled Pugash. "It's gone mad!"

"What, what?" stammered Hatvan, his head muddled by such an abrupt reveille. "Clock, hey? What's it been up to?"

Pugash hustled his disheveled commander across the square. The shoemaker and the fishmonger crouched behind the horse trough.

"There! Look at it!" Pugash pointed at the clock tower.

Indeed, both hands of the clock were spinning like a pinwheel. Hatvan blinked. The whirling hands were making him dizzy. He pronounced his considered opinion.

"It's broken. Lieutenant Pugash, go fix it. Hup, hup!"

The barber made no attempt to obey. The shoemaker gasped in horror; the fishmonger shrank closer to the protection of the horse trough. Hatvan, fully awake, gulped and choked and put a hand to the hilt of his saber, though trembling too violently to draw the blade.

A corpse-white figure had appeared at a corner of the tower. A dull glow hung about the ghostly shape as it slowly spread what seemed to be wide, fluttering wings. Anguished, bloodcurdling wails rose from the ghastly form.

Hatvan froze. The clock had stopped whirling, but now the

figure halted in front of it, wings uplifted, wailing all the louder. Hatvan stared, unable to tear his eyes from the monstrous apparition.

Finally, the general gritted his teeth and shook himself into action, bringing to bear a seasoned officer's ability to make cool-headed decisions in the face of mortal danger.

"Retreat!" he commanded.

16

The Haunting of the Town Hall

HE TOWN WATCH made a strategic withdrawal to the inn. Hatvan led his troops with such energy that he outdistanced them and was first to tumble into the taproom. Once there, he had presence of mind to draw his saber and brandish it ferociously. The terrified barber, fishmonger, and shoemaker babbled among themselves while Hatvan stood fast, eager to repel any spectral attackers. The commotion roused Mr. Farkas, who came groggily to inquire what the devil the racket was about.

"Devil, indeed!" cried Hatvan. "There's a ghost in the clock tower."

"Why?" Farkas yawned. "Who'd put a goat there?"

"Ghost! Ghost, you fool!" Hatvan shouted. "Horrible! The whole town's in danger!"

"Let it wait." Farkas cast an eye on the general's unfinished bottle. "There's spirits of one kind and spirits of another. Deal with it in the morning, when your head's clearer."

"My head's clear as ever it's been," put in the shoemaker. "I saw the ghost. We all did. It's there, sure enough."

"Inform the mayor. Straightaway." Hatvan had recaptured his sense of command. "Lieutenant Pugash, fetch him here. On the double!"

"Go outside?" The barber recoiled. "And that pestilential emanation still abroad? You're the commander. Fetch him yourself."

"Insubordination!" Hatvan shook his saber at Pugash, who had planted his feet with the clear intention of not moving them. He turned to the fishmonger. "Sergeant Sobako. Forward march!"

The fishmonger refused point blank, the shoemaker likewise. Hatvan, finding himself with a mutiny on his hands and being outnumbered by the mutineers, chose to avoid court-martialing them. He ordered Farkas to carry out the mission.

"Why me?" protested Farkas, by now persuaded something weird and possibly dangerous was afoot. "None of my business. I'm a civilian."

The first thing, Hatvan decided, was to find out if the ghost still held the clock tower. He called a council of war, including Farkas as representative of the townsfolk, and all enthusiastically agreed: The best individual for the task was the potboy.

The lad was accordingly rooted out of his cot and, still half asleep, given hasty instructions to observe the tower, then was booted out of the door, which Mr. Farkas bolted securely behind him.

Hatvan set up his command post at the table. Before he had concluded a major offensive against the sausages, there came a pounding at the door and the scout was cautiously admitted.

"What's the fuss?" The potboy, tousled and bemused, glanced at the grim faces around him. "I didn't see anything at all."

Hearing this, Hatvan boldly sallied forth to look at the tower. As reported, it was unoccupied. The ghost had vanished.

Nevertheless, next morning, at the general's insistence, Mayor Pumpa called an emergency council meeting. The barber, fishmonger, and shoemaker testified to what they had seen. Sharpnack sent Fibich into the tower, but the clerk returned to state nothing amiss and no sign there had been any spectral presence.

"Ah, yes, well, all very odd." Mayor Pumpa had never previously dealt with a ghost and was uncertain what administrative procedure to follow, since apparently no law had been broken. "In any case, it's gone away. So, that's the end of that."

"Oh, no, it isn't," Podskalny retorted. "Don't try to wiggle out of your duty. Take firm action. Suppose it comes back. I won't put up with a ghost. It could be bad for the cloth business."

"Civil disorder is what it might lead to," Sharpnack declared. "There's already gossip all over town. The matter must be settled immediately. The first thing you do, Pumpa, is deny that anything happened, then issue official reassurance it won't happen again."

"If I might offer a suggestion," Fibich ventured, while Sharpnack groaned, "go see if the thing reappears. If it does, you'll have a better idea what you're denying."

Mayor Pumpa blanched. Sharpnack looked grimmer than usual. Podskalny, wrought up more by ghostly influence on his trade than fear of the ghost itself, sided with the clerk, as did Hatvan. The mayor reluctantly admitted that the august presence of the council among the citizenry would produce a soothing effect and convened a meeting for midnight in the square.

A little while before the hour, when the council, including the town watch and Constable Shicker, gathered by the horse trough, half of Greater Dunitsa already waited uneasily around the town hall—the other half preferring to wait behind locked doors and shuttered windows. The tower was empty.

"Just as I expected." Mayor Pumpa heaved a grateful sigh.

"A temporary phenomenon, merely drifting by, as it were. Well, then, good night, all."

No sooner had he spoken than the clock's hands began to spin madly. Gasps of horror shuddered through the crowd for, a moment later, the gruesome specter rose up, keening and shrieking, beating its menacing wings. A number of townsfolk suddenly remembered chores to do at home. Others milled around the dignitaries, jostling them and yelling for something to be done on the spot. Yielding to popular demand, Mayor Pumpa drew himself up in the full authority of his office:

"General Hatvan, take your people and storm the tower."

"None of that storming business," cried the shoemaker, with the enthusiastic assent of his comrades-in-arms. "We're the town watch, aren't we? And that's exactly what we're doing: watching the town."

Mayor Pumpa rounded on the constable. "Shicker, arrest that ghost."

"Not my perimeters of duty." The constable had begun looking bilious. "Incorporeated manifestations don't fall within my jurisdicational purviews. A dogfight, a burglary—I'd be there in a flash."

Mayor Pumpa noticed that Sharpnack and Podskalny were sloping away in the direction of their houses, and Hatvan was nowhere to be seen. Giving the situation his most careful consideration, he shouldered through the crowd, pausing only to declare:

"Meeting adjourned."

From her vantage point in the clock tower, Rizka smiled with satisfaction. Draped in one of Mrs. Pumpa's night-gowns—the mayor's wife was a woman of generous dimension—she flapped her arms a few more times and, for good measure, let out some especially blood-chilling shrieks. The lantern she used to produce the eerie glow was flickering out and, after one last encore, she ended her public appearance for the night. Pleased, but a little tired from so much scream-ing, as well as turning the gears of the clock, she hid until the square emptied, then crept down and flitted home to Petzel and the kittens.

Chief Councilor Sharpnack's prediction of civil disorder showed signs of coming true. The ghost appeared again the following midnight; next morning, some tradesmen refused to open their shops; householders cowered indoors. The more blustery citizens rallied around the horse trough, shouting for the mayor to get rid of the ghost—which had no doubt wan-dered in from another town, certainly not a local spirit. A cou-ple of fistfights broke out for no reason other than general crankiness; Constable Shicker sustained a black eye in the line of duty and had to withdraw to Farkas's inn for treatment.

Urged by Mr. Podskalny, Mayor Pumpa offered a reward to anyone who stayed in the tower to grapple with the spectre. The sum, however, was either too small or the danger too great; no one volunteered.

At the same time, Sharpnack found a tangled skein of garter snakes in his bedroom slippers. Mayor Pumpa was shocked out of his appetite by a large turtle on his breakfast tray. Podskalny encountered a troop of frogs frolicking amid his bolts of cloth.

"A plague! The ghost brought it on!" Podskalny burst out to his fellow council members. "Closer and closer! Attacking us in hearth, home, and merchandise!"

The most mysterious intrusion was discovered on the third morning. The council, assembling for yet another emergency meeting, stared horrified at what had been drawn in the middle of the table.

"The ghost again!" Podskalny flung up his hands. "Through locked doors! In the bosom of our administrative chamber!"

"Is no place sacred?" exclaimed Sharpnack.

Hatvan backed away. "Mystical signs, hey? Don't get too close to them."

"They're cats." Fibich squinted through his spectacles. "Yes, unmistakably cats. Five, and some kind of writing."

"What are they doing here?" Mayor Pumpa scratched his head. "Gentlemen, I confess I'm baffled."

"We all know that," muttered Podskalny.

"It occurs to me," Fibich dared to put in, "when you're sick, you consult a doctor."

"Certainly not Pugash." Sharpnack snorted. "What's that to do with anything?"

"The principle's the same," Fibich said. "Expert advice. A professional opinion. From someone who should know about ghosts, hauntings, weird goings on—trade secrets, as it were —and prescribe a treatment."

"An expert in weirdness?" retorted Sharpnack. "You maundering rodent, where do you propose finding one, if there's even such a thing?"

The chief councilor broke off; his fellow members glanced at each other as the same thought filtered into their minds. Mayor Pumpa nodded, with much uneasiness:

"Get the Gypsy."

Escorted by Constable Shicker, Rizka sauntered into the chamber. Sharpnack glared. The last time he had been at close quarters with her, he had been plastered with honey and feathers; and he anxiously touched his nose to make sure it was securely in its proper place. Giving Sharpnack a pleasant smile, Rizka listened to Mayor Pumpa's explanations, then went to study the drawings and inscriptions she herself had made during the night.

"Mustard?" Rizka dipped a finger into the yellow substance she had used to depict the cats and sniffed it. "This is more serious than I thought."

"Who cares if it's mustard or—or caper sauce?" Sharpnack caught himself before he said "chicken stuffing." Thanks to the illustrious Dr. Skizzarkus, he had regained his taste for his favorite dish, but it was still a touchy point with him. "I want a straight answer. Can you get rid of this ghost or whatever it is?"

"Difficult." Rizka pursed her lips. "Very difficult. But possible. The first thing—"

"The first thing is the price," Podskalny interrupted. "How much will you try to squeeze out of us?"

"To save the town? Let me see." Rizka thought for a moment. "I'll charge—not a penny. It's my civic duty."

"Don't tell me civic duty, you Gypsy swindler," exclaimed Sharpnack. "You're up to no good. You're trying to cheat us in some way. I'll tell you this: If you don't rid us of that ghastly thing, I'll come down on you so hard, I'll see to it you'll never set foot in this town. I'll ruin you—"

"Please, Chief Councilor, don't say anything to upset her at this crucial moment. She's made a most unselfish offer." Mayor Pumpa, who had braced himself for an assault on the municipal treasury, beamed at Rizka. "Well, well, my dear young lady, go right about your work. We'll just tiptoe out and leave you in privacy."

"Not that simple." Rizka put her little finger to her ear. "It's telling me what all this means. There's an essential requirement.

"I'll need five cats, all mustard-colored," she went on. "I have to bring them here to the council chamber."

"No shortage of them, hey?" said Hatvan. "That beast of yours, he's made sure there's plenty in town."

Rizka shook her head. "They have to be young kittens. All born the same day from the same litter."

"What's the likelihood?" Mayor Pumpa groaned. "None! We're doomed!"

"This is my responsibility," said Rizka. "Leave it to me. There are a few other requirements. You'll all follow them exactly."

"And you," said Sharpnack, "you've been warned. If you're trifling with us, I'll make you wish you'd never been born."

"I'd never wish that," said Rizka.

Close to midnight, as Rizka ordered, the entire council gathered in the chamber, with Fibich and Constable Shicker attending. Also present, by Rizka's instructions: Mrs. Pumpa and the girls; Sofiya, brightly eager; the gorgeous Esperanza, superb at any hour; the adorable Galanta and Galatea, half asleep on their feet; little Roswitha, fretful. Though late spring, the air was nippy. A candelabra burned in the middle of the table, but Rizka had strictly forbidden any fire in the fireplace.

"Gypsy wretch." Sharpnack blew on his fingers. "I knew it. She's diddled us again and made us look a pack of fools."

Rizka, with her exquisite sense of the dramatic moment, waited some time longer outside in the hall, then strode in purposefully, halted at the table, and tipped over the basket she carried.

"It took some doing," Rizka declared, "but here they are."

The five kittens rolled out. Mayor Pumpa gaped; Podskalny and the others murmured in astonishment. The girls, little Roswitha loudest of all, immediately went "Ooh" and "Aah," but Rizka motioned for silence. She handed a kitten to each of the mayor's daughters, adding a wink for Sofiya.

"Hold them carefully. Gently," she ordered, as if it needed saying, for the girls were lovingly stroking their fur, tickling them under the chin, while little Roswitha, cooing in rapture, planted sweet kisses between her kitten's ears.

"All of you stand back," Rizka went on. "It's midnight. The ghost should be in the tower. They're creatures of habit, you know. Very predictable."

Muttering to herself, tracing mysterious signs in the air, she at last took up one of the candles. With a grand gesture, she flung it into the empty fireplace.

A blinding flash and muffled explosion set the onlookers back on their heels. Hatvan, yelling that the ghost had attacked, lunged for the door. Podskalny ducked under the table. The girls screamed; the kittens sneezed as smoke billowed from the fireplace—Rizka had packed it with Big Franko's gunpowder—and a pungent cloud drifted through the chamber.

"Done." Rizka dusted off her hands. "That's the end of your ghost."

"I'll want more than your say-so," retorted Sharpnack. "Gone? You'll have me to deal with if it isn't. Prove it."

"I guarantee it won't be back," said Rizka. "But, to make sure: Fibich, go look at the tower." The clerk hurried out and moments later returned to declare it empty. The spectre had vanished without a trace that it had ever been there.

"Most effective, I do admit." Mayor Pumpa still trembled from the shock. "The town—yes, we can all say it—the town is officially grateful." He turned to the girls. "Now, my darlings, give the nice Gypsy lady her animals and she'll be on her way."

Little Roswitha burst into tears. "Not give kitty. Mine." Her sisters likewise refused and wailed louder than the ghost. Before the mayor could extract the kittens from his daughters' loving clutches, Rizka raised a hand.

"I forgot to tell you," she said to Mayor Pumpa. "They have to keep the kittens, all of them. Feed them well; give them the best of care. Otherwise," she warned, as Sofiya grinned at her, "the ghost will come back worse than ever."

"Do as she says, Pumpa," the mayor's wife ordered. "I've had my fill of midnight screaming; we've enough at home already. Five extra mouths to feed? We'll afford it somehow, even if I have to cut down on your dinners."

"Of course, of course, my dear," the mayor said, appalled at the prospect. "We might, instead, raise the price of cheese to make up the difference."

"No," said Rizka. "The town's been saved from horrible danger. The council should grant those kittens a lifetime pension."

"Eh? Yes, well, I suppose we should," said Mayor Pumpa. "Does anyone object?"

"Better not," Rizka said under her breath.

"Unanimously agreed," the mayor declared when no voice was raised. "My goodness, that doesn't often happen. Fibich, make a special note of it."

Romance in Greater Dunitsa

THE PHANTOM never came back. Hatvan's dauntless behavior grew more dauntless in hindsight. Yet, horrible and terrifying as it was, the folk of Greater Dunitsa rather missed their town ghost. It had become, during its brief appearance, a local celebrity, and was talked about like an absent family member off on a long voyage, with a hint of yearning and fond hope for its return.

The kittens thrived; the Pumpa girls doted on them. Rizka and Sofiya never breathed a word of how they had rigged their scheme. Nevertheless, a wispy impression, a vague breeze wafted among the mayor's daughters: Rizka could work wonders if she felt like it. So, at her pupil's entreaty, she accepted a new client.

"I'll tell you a secret," Sofiya whispered. "Esperanza—she's in love. With Lorins Podskalny."

"I know already." Rizka easily guessed, even before Sofiya brought her sister to the *vardo*, what the mayor's eldest daughter had in mind. The heady influence of spring in Greater Dunitsa put the town's young people in a frenzy; sweethearts were getting married right and left. Poor Fibich could barely keep up with certificates and registrations. Mayor Pumpa spent a good portion of his days performing wedding ceremonies, but never one for Esperanza and Lorins.

"My father hates Mr. Podskalny, and Mr. Podskalny hates my father. I think it has something to do with cheese. And rags." Tears smudged Esperanza's cheeks; her nose was a delicate pink as the result of sniffling. She managed, however, to look incredibly gorgeous and desperately miserable at the same time.

"*O Podskalny, Podskalny,*" she declaimed, arms outspread— she had been well taught elocution and the classics by Mr. Mellish—

Wherefore art thou Podskalny?
Deny thy father and refuse thy name. . . .
And I'll no longer be a Pumpa.

"You're a Pumpa, like it or not," said Rizka. "That won't work."

"What's to be done?" cried Esperanza. "We thought of eloping—"

"Run off?" Sofiya burst out. "With your clothes in a bundle at the end of a stick? You could never come home again, you know."

"Unthinkable," agreed Rizka. "No need for it. Now, tell me: Your heart's truly set on Lorins?"

"We'd give our lives for each other." Esperanza flung a hand to her bosom and broke into tears again. "We'll die together if we must. Could you mix a fatal potion?"

"A little too permanent." Fervent devotion never failed to touch Rizka, but she also stayed practical-minded about it. "Anyhow, stop blubbering. It doesn't help. There has to be another way."

"I beg you!" Esperanza sobbed. "Tell me what it is."

"Be quiet," Sofiya said, recognizing the distant gaze in Rizka's eyes, "can't you see she's thinking?"

Esperanza sank down on a stool and blew her nose with surprisingly loud honkings. To console her, Petzel jumped to her lap and purred sympathetically. Rizka paced back and forth and at last turned to the snuffling Esperanza:

"First, does anyone know about you and Lorins?"

Esperanza shook her head. "Only Sofiya."

"Good. But," Rizka warned, "I can't guarantee results. With love affairs, no telling how things turn out. If you're willing to do as I say, it's worth trying."

"We'll dare anything," Esperanza declared. "Whatever the sacrifice—"

"Yes, yes, that's all well and good," Rizka said. "Just pull yourself together and listen carefully."

When Rizka finished her instructions, Esperanza gratefully embraced her and stepped out of the *vardo* more hopefully than when she first stepped in. Sofiya hung back.

"That's what you want them to do?" she whispered. "They could really get themselves in trouble."

Rizka patted her pupil's head. "Your sister may weep like a drainspout, but I'd guess she's braver than she looks. She'll start things moving pretty briskly."

The Sunday promenade began more expansively than usual. The dignitaries had packed away their winter clothing and got out their springtime finery. In the sunny afternoon, the mayor, Mrs. Pumpa, and their darlings as always led the clockwise procession around the square. Mayor Pumpa, who had been given credit—and not refused it—for the expulsion of the ghost, beamed and tipped his hat, acknowledging respectful greetings from the counter-clockwise strollers.

Mayor Pumpa did not notice that his eldest daughter no longer walked with the rest of the family. Murmurs of astonishment rippled among the onlookers. The promenaders had shifted their attention to the horse trough.

The loitering ragamuffins whooped gleefully and made

rude shame-on-you motions with their fingers. The mouths of the adorable twins turned into identical *O*'s. Mrs. Pumpa went pale, tilted back on her heels, and nearly dropped little Roswitha. It was all Sofiya could do to prop up her swooning mother from the rear.

At the horse trough, in full view of Greater Dunitsa and all the world, the beautiful Esperanza Pumpa and the handsome Lorins Podskalny stood face to face, hand in hand, lost in each other's adoring eyes. Deliciously scandalized, the promenaders in both directions stopped in their tracks.

Mayor Pumpa, roaring like a lion seeing the cub of its heart beset by a hyena, headed for the couple as fast as his bulk would allow. Doting father though he was, his dear daughter in company with a Podskalny—the two, in fact, seemed ready to embrace—was more than paternal flesh and blood could bear.

"Have you gone mad? Have you lost all sense of propriety?" Mayor Pumpa seized his daughter's arm. "Home! This instant!"

He propelled Esperanza toward the protective wing of her mother, who had stopped swooning long enough to follow her husband. "Mrs. Pumpa! Control your child!"

The mayor then focused his outrage and indignation on Lorins Podskalny and began smacking the young man about the ears with the brim of his hat.

"Pumpa! You dare to strike my son?" Mr. Podskalny, lumbering up a few seconds later, shouldered Lorins aside. "See to your girl. Shameless hussy! Luring, enticing an innocent young Podskalny!"

"Don't tell me luring and enticing," Mayor Pumpa flung back. "Your sprig's the enticer. Keep that tomcat away. Lock him up."

Mr. Podskalny and Mayor Pumpa would have come to blows except for their wives hauling at their coattails. The two dignitaries allowed themselves to be dragged apart.

"There! That's for you, Podskalny!" Mayor Pumpa shouted from a safe distance, tearing his handkerchief from his sleeve and flapping it full length. "Shoddy rags!"

"And this for you, Pumpa!" Mr. Podskalny thrust two fingers at his nostrils until they were in danger of vanishing. "Stinking cheese!"

By then, however, a number of townsfolk—half of them allies of Mayor Pumpa, the other half supporters of Mr. Podskalny—began their own scuffle, swinging fists and jabbing elbows. Mr. Karras, the corn dealer, on good terms with Pumpa and Podskalny alike, was caught between the combatants and accidentally received a punch on the nose, which so distressed the usually sweet-tempered Karras that he called down a plague on both their houses and their friends as well.

Blustering, sputtering the old familiar insults, the mayor and the cloth merchant were nudged, shoved, and cajoled into going home with their respective offspring. The rest, exhausted, retreated to nurse their bruises.

Those onlookers who had no allegiance one way or the other waited hopefully to see if something else would erupt. Since it did not, they went home themselves.

After a restless night, still shaken by the incident at the horse trough, Mayor Pumpa intended giving his daughter a stern talking-to as soon as he fortified himself with an ample breakfast.

He had just finished buttoning his shirt when Mrs. Pumpa flew in, lace cap and apron askew, wringing her hands, a wild look in her eyes. At first, the mayor feared his wife had burned the bacon.

"There, there, my dear, calm yourself," he said. "What's amiss?"

"Gone!" Mrs. Pumpa shook him by the collar and wailed in his ear. "Our darling Sprinzi's gone!"

"Eh? Where?" Mayor Pumpa stiffened. "What's happened?"

"The girls didn't see her this morning. She's not slept in her bed," Mrs. Pumpa blurted. "She's disappeared!"

Something between a growl of fury and a groan of dismay burst through the mayor's clenched teeth. "Podskalny! He has a hand in this. With his whelp! Skulduggery! I can smell it!"

Without bothering to put on his jacket and cravat, or swallow a bite of breakfast, Mayor Pumpa rumbled downstairs, stormed through the front door, and launched himself in the direction of the cloth merchant's house.

He had only reached the middle of the square when he stopped short. Podskalny, likewise in shirtsleeves, with a distraught Mrs. Podskalny at his heels, was making straight for Mayor Pumpa.

"Where's my son?" Podskalny bellowed. "You're behind this in some way."

"Where's my daughter?" Mayor Pumpa retorted. "What have you cooked up with that offspring of yours?"

"Both run away?" cried Mrs. Podskalny.

"Eloped?" Mrs. Pumpa, leaving the little ones in Sofiya's care, had come in time to hear this last comment. "Perish the thought!"

Mayor Pumpa thrust his jaw at Mr. Podskalny. "Your whippersnapper—you put him up to it. Make off with my girl and add a Pumpa to your family of ragpickers. Raise yourself into high society—"

"With a Pumpa?" the cloth merchant flung back. "I should graft cheese onto my family tree?"

"Stop it, you two," ordered Mrs. Podskalny. "If they've run away together, go fetch them back."

"From where?" demanded Mrs. Pumpa. "You can't fetch them until you find them."

At that moment, by one of her carefully managed coincidences, Rizka stepped from behind the horse trough, where she had been conveniently lounging with Bagrat and a couple of his fellow urchins.

"I saw them just a little while ago." She motioned toward

the hills. "They were going to Ali Baba's cave—that's what I call it, anyhow. Yes, I know the place exactly."

"Cave?" wailed Mrs. Podskalny. "They'll be eaten by bears! Devoured by wolves!"

"Lost forever!" wailed Mrs. Pumpa.

"You might have a chance of finding them—if it isn't too late and you don't get lost yourselves," Ritza warned.

"Take us there." Mr. Podskalny clasped his hands. "I beg you!"

"I have a lot to do this morning," Rizka said. "But—all right, I'll show you the way."

The Runaways

MAYOR PUMPA, with unusual decisiveness, shouted for Constable Shicker, ordering him to rouse Hatvan and the town watch in case bears and wolves had to be dealt with. Rizka dispatched Bagrat and his cronies to fetch Big Franko in all haste.

As soon as they got wind of this turn of events, a swelling crowd of townsfolk outfitted themselves with torches, coils of rope, spades, pickaxes, and sandwiches. Fibich, who could not resist visiting the cavern again, tossed aside his papers and trotted out to join Rizka. Sharpnack sacrificed a role in the search party to remain dutifully in the council chamber, ready to take full authority should Mayor Pumpa meet with a regrettably fatal accident.

With Rizka serving as guide, and General Hatvan hup-hupping in a vain attempt to make all march in good order, the straggling procession scrambled up to the hills. Reaching the cave, Rizka glanced back at the enthusiastic rescuers tripping over roots and stumbling through the underbrush, and ordered most of them to stay outside; Hatvan posted himself at the cavern's mouth to make sure they did. Torches in hand, Big Franko and Fibich followed Rizka through the rock-lined passages. The clerk's eyes brightened to see the walls and domed ceilings glittering as magically as he remembered them. Mrs. Pumpa and Mrs. Podskalny went arm in arm to encourage each other, their husbands trembling after them.

"Watch where you step," Rizka warned. "No telling what might happen in a place like this." She pointed to the mineral deposits hanging from the ceiling. "If one of those ever came loose—why, for all you know, Lori and Sprinzi could have been squashed under a pile of rocks."

"No, no!" burst out Mrs. Pumpa. "Horrible! Not my Sprinzi!"

"Not my dear Lori!" echoed Mrs. Podskalny.

"Well, they did disobey you," said Rizka. "If they had an accident, they brought it on themselves."

"Who cares about that now!" cried Mrs. Pumpa. "If only they're alive—"

"We'll have to keep searching. We'll find out, one way or another." The farther Rizka led them into the passages, the more distraught the two mothers became and the faces of the mayor and the cloth merchant all the more grim, especially since Rizka pointed out every possible hazard that could have befallen the runaways.

"Here's one of the worst." Rizka beckoned the parents to the pool of steaming mud. "Very dangerous"—she glanced back at Fibich—"I know of people who fell into it. I'd rather not tell you what became of them."

"My Sprinzi!" Mrs. Pumpa gasped as she stared at the menacing pool. "Could she have slipped—?"

"And my dear Lori jumped in to save her?" Mrs. Podskalny clapped her hands to her cheeks. "Brave boy, that would be just like him to do that. And now—both lost!"

"It's true they were upset because of you and paying no attention where they were stepping," Rizka said. "Even so, I'm sure that didn't happen."

"But it might have," wailed Mrs. Pumpa, shaken by the dire prospect that Rizka had planted in her imagination. "Suppose it did?" She wheeled around to seize Mayor Pumpa by his shirt front. "See what you've done? You've driven the poor child to desperation! You were too stern; you know she has a sensitive nature. And then you go smacking the lad with your hat—"

"That's right!" Mr. Podskalny burst out. "Who set off the whole business? Pumpa!"

"What about you?" Mrs. Podskalny shook a finger in her husband's face. "You're no better, with your blather about cheese on the family tree. No wonder poor Lori ran off."

"So don't blame me, you upstart ragpicker," Mayor Pumpa exclaimed. "It's your fault—"

"I don't care whose fault it is," Mrs. Pumpa broke in. "I'd give anything in the world to see my darling Sprinzi safe and sound."

"I, too," moaned Mrs. Podskalny, "if only my dear Lori were alive and well."

"Whatever they've done," Mr. Podskalny declared, "I'll be the first to forgive them."

"Oh, no, you won't," Mayor Pumpa countered. "I forgave them already, before we came here. I neglected to mention it."

"That's all very fine," said Rizka, "but there's something else they want."

"They'll have it," said Mr. Podskalny. "Whatever it is."

"Indeed, they will," Mayor Pumpa added. "Ah—what is it?"

"They want to get married," said Rizka.

"Good heavens, is that all?" Mrs. Pumpa, ready to give in to some dreadful demand, heaved a sigh of relief. "Then let them do it. They needn't have gone and lost themselves in the bowels of the earth."

"Of course, let them," said Mrs. Podskalny, equally relieved. "I'd rather see them married than eaten by bears or at the bottom of a boiling mud puddle."

"If I'd known they were desperate enough to risk life and limb in this horrible place—" Mr. Podskalny ruefully shook his head. "I never thought they'd go this far. If we find them— yes, yes, they'll have my blessings."

"And mine. Double. Triple," Mayor Pumpa asserted. "More blessings than you'd ever give, you windbag."

"Don't try to outbless me, you waffler," retorted Podskalny. "Just hope we're not too late."

"I think you're right on time," Rizka said under her breath.

While their wives tried to console each other and Podskalny and Mayor Pumpa bickered over whose blessings were greater, Rizka motioned briefly. Hand in hand, the runaways appeared from behind a row of stone icicles.

Mrs. Pumpa and Mrs. Podskalny, squealing, stammering, weeping in joyful astonishment, flew to embrace them. The mayor and the cloth merchant flung their arms around all four, with everyone in such a tangle that Rizka could not sort out which child was being hugged by which parent.

"My dear boy, you had us frightened out of our wits." Mr. Podskalny finally unclutched his son and allowed him to breathe. "Your poor mother's beside herself. Whatever possessed you to run off to this dank hole in the ground?"

"Better to face the dangers here than be separated from my beloved Sprinzi." Lorins laid a hand on his breast and drew himself up to his full height. His mustache curled gallantly as he looked squarely at his parent. "We wished to be alone, to find some means of reconciling our two great houses—both alike in dignity."

"He speaks so well, the brave boy," Mrs. Podskalny whispered to Mrs. Pumpa. "With a head for business, too."

"We wanted your blessing on our marriage," Esperanza happily put in. "Which you've given."

"Yes, well, that's when we feared you were lost forever," Podskalny replied. He clapped Lorins on the shoulder. "But now, my lad, home you go and forget all this nonsense."

"You, too, Sprinzi," said Mayor Pumpa. "You're safe and well, darling child. That's the end of it."

"What do you mean, the end of it?" If Esperanza had shown a tendency to spout tears in Rizka's *vardo*, her lovely eyes now flashed dangerously. "You agreed we could marry."

"Ah—perhaps so," admitted Mr. Podskalny, as Mayor Pumpa nodded support. "Things are said in the heat of the moment, you understand. Later, on calm reflection—"

"Is this my father whom I hear?" Lorins's noble brow darkened. "A merchant fails to keep his word? A chief magistrate breaks his promise? Behavior unworthy of a Podskalny—and a Pumpa!"

"Don't worry about it. Look"—Rizka cocked a thumb at Mrs. Pumpa and Mrs. Podskalny, heads together, chattering back and forth—"they're already talking gowns and refreshments. Besides," she added to the cloth merchant and the mayor, "you both approved. Right out in public. We all heard you. Fibich is a notary, so that makes it official.

"If word gets around that you backed out," Rizka continued, "Podskalny, I don't think your customers will be too eager to deal with you. The mayor might be run out of office by angry citizens. People like to see lovers united."

"Ahem, yes, so they do, so they do." Mayor Pumpa chewed his lips. "Very well, I give my permission—for the sake of the youngsters and the good of the public at large."

"And the cloth trade," said Podskalny. "All right, so be it. Your hand, Pumpa."

"Here it is, Podskalny." The mayor reached out his own hand and firmly shook the cloth merchant's. "I'll even go so far as to say I'm delighted."

"Not half as delighted as I am," replied Podskalny.

While the future in-laws, the sweethearts, Fibich, and the others trooped from the cave, Big Franko winked at Rizka. "*Chiriklo*, you little Gypsy bird," he said, "I won't ask what all you had to do with this, but I know you had a finger in it." The blacksmith chuckled and wagged his head. "Without Pumpa and Podskalny at each other's throats—I'm afraid things won't be quite the same."

19

The Wedding Party

MISS LETTA, commissioned to make the wedding gown, created one as magnificent as the bride. Mr. Farkas, activating his entire catering staff—the potboy and the scullery maid—set about preparing the wedding refreshments. Since he was famous for the elegance of his arrangements, the success of the grand occasion was assured. Mayor Pumpa insisted on the honor of giving his daughter away, so the question came up: Who to perform the ceremony? Sharpnack was better suited to preside over a funeral or a hanging. Instead of the chief councilor, the mayor authorized Fibich, as notary and town clerk, to conduct the formalities in the council chamber.

Greater Dunitsa had never witnessed such a reception. The

sun beamed lavishly, as if hired especially for the event. The puffy clouds lazily drifting over the square looked like part of the decorations, the streamers, festoons, and bunting Mr. Farkas had strung up at the front of the town hall.

Amid tables of food and drink tastefully circling the horse trough, the wedding cake—a masterpiece of confection by Mr. Chudra, the baker—towered in regal grandeur on its own pedestal, with Mr. Chudra himself in proud attendance to shoo away intruding flies and yellowjackets.

As the wedding party emerged, the town band, under the baton of Mr. Karras, the corn dealer, began trumpeting and tromboning enough to deafen themselves and the spectators. Sharpnack, not to be outdone by a cake, opened his pigeon coops, and the birds wheeled festively above the rooftops.

The more distinguished guests, having embraced the bride and groom, embraced the refeshments. The less distinguished townsfolk cheered at the top of their voices, hoping for a distribution of leftovers. Despite the entreaties of the Pumpa girls, Rizka had not been formally invited, but she was there semi-officially—to the extent that no one chased her away—with Big Franko at her side in the front rank of the onlookers.

Mayor Pumpa, at his most expansive in a brocaded waist-coat, and Mr. Podskalny, in equal finery, stood together accepting congratulations and admiring the efforts of Mr. Farkas.

"I'll say this, Pumpa," observed Mr. Podskalny, "I commend you. You've laid it on handsomely."

"Thank you, Podskalny," said Mayor Pumpa, banishing to the distant recesses of his mind the prospect of four more daughters to see expensively married. "No skimping, no holding back. Only the best, as my Sprinzi deserves."

"Indeed," Podskalny said, in a tone suggesting that his son likewise deserved the best and no doubt more. "You've gone all the way. Pies, pastries, meats. And here, this fine spread of cheese. From your own shop, eh? The real thing, I suppose. It wouldn't be second-rate—"

"What's that mean?" Mayor Pumpa bristled. "Suppose? Real thing? Second-rate—I could ask the same about that rig you've got on."

No one, not even Rizka, was exactly certain what happened next. In discussions later—and ever after as permanent town gossip—nothing could be agreed on.

Possibly one of Sharpnack's pigeons swooped down to peck at the refreshments and Mayor Pumpa pulled out his handkerchief to chase off the impudent bird. Or perhaps a yellowjacket flew up Mr. Podskalny's nose and the cloth merchant deployed a finger to get it out.

In any case, at Podskalny's gesture, the mayor shook his handkerchief ferociously. "Want to talk cheese, do you? Then let's talk rags, you pushcart scavenger!"

Podskalny's wattles turned crimson and he gnashed his

teeth. "How dare you—you cheese-faker! Cheese, cheese, cheese! Gorgonzola! Roquefort! Limburger!"

"Rags!" Mayor Pumpa bellowed. "Shoddy rags! Cheapjack trash! Tatters! Moth-eaten junk!"

The dignitaries flung themselves at each other, the mayor trying to throttle Podskalny—with difficulty because of the diameter of the cloth merchant's neck—and Podskalny pummeling the mayor's brocaded waistcoat. Clutching at lapels, cravats, or an ear when available, locked in breathless combat, they tumbled to the ground and rolled on the cobblestones.

The guests cried out in dismay, hastily turning up jacket collars and draping shawls over their heads, not because of the epic battle between the town's leading citizens. Rain had suddenly begun bucketing down.

Intent on the refeshments, no one had glanced at the clouds, which had so quickly changed from cottony puffs to ominous black mountains. Within the instant, the sky opened like a giant trapdoor. Sheets of water flooded the square; the streets turned into rivers and canals. As Fibich would later determine from the archives, Greater Dunitsa had never known such a deluge.

Even as the tide rose, Mayor Pumpa and Mr. Podskalny kept flailing away at each other. Meantime, the pedestal with its wedding cake overturned, and Mr. Chudra's masterpiece floated like a majestic white ship under full sail. The wedding couple, happy but soaking wet, headed back into the town hall. The band scattered, protectively clutching their instruments; the onlookers raced for cover.

"Look there!" Starting for a sheltering doorway, Rizka halted and seized Big Franko's arm. The water had reached well above her ankles, but she stood rooted to the spot. "He was right!"

Mr. Karpath's boat bore steadily across the square. Seeing his yard awash, the carpenter had knocked away the supporting blocks and launched his vessel into the street. The town urchins, drawn to this new entertainment, gathered to skid the craft on its course like a seagoing sled.

Petzel perched at the bow as if he were a ship's figurehead. Mr. Karpath, wild triumph blazing in his eyes, kicked up his heels to dance a sailor's hornpipe.

"Make way, you lubbers!" he shouted in his best nautical voice. "On to glory!"

The craft slewed around. Rizka and Big Franko hurried to keep the boat from foundering on the reefs of floating refreshment tables. Mr. Karpath capered victoriously, waving his captain's cap and roaring "Avast and belay! On to glory!"

Mr. Chudra's wedding cake bobbed its majestic way. Braving the storm, Sharpnack's pigeons flocked around it, filling their beaks. General Hatvan, from the doorway of the inn, waved his saber and bawled for the town watch, nowhere to be found. Mayor Pumpa and Mr. Podskalny, still locked in combat, floundered in the water, spouting like whales, yelling "Cheese!" and "Rags!

"Afraid things wouldn't be the same?" observed Rizka, as she and Big Franko clung to the side of the boat. "I'd say those two are back to normal."

The Zipple

THE DOWNPOUR stopped as quickly as it had come, leaving Greater Dunitsa none the worse, if anything, all the better. The newlyweds were divinely happy. The mothers-in-law became bosom friends, bonded by the ridiculous behavior of their husbands. Mayor Pumpa and Mr. Podskalny made their sopping way home, each convinced he had taught the other a good sharp lesson. The townsfolk had something new and delightful to gossip about. Mr. Karpath was the only one disappointed; he had hoped for a bigger flood.

"But," said Rizka, as she and Big Franko helped the carpenter drag the boat to his lumberyard, "you can't please everybody."

However, before the town could settle down properly and

discuss the disaster from all angles, Greater Dunitsa faced its annual attack: the dreaded Zipple.

The Zipple always began in late summer: a soft, cajoling little breeze from the south, a trickle of air hardly enough to ripple the placid water of the horse trough. It should have been pleasant. It was horrible. For one reason: It never let up. The Zipple was relentless.

"Like someone coming at you every minute of the day and being cheerful," Big Franko said as he and Rizka were trudging back from doctoring a lame colt, "you finally want to grab them by the collar and shake them.

"You, *chiriklo*, be glad of your Gypsy blood. You're immune. The rest of the town goes a little crazy."

"How can you tell the difference?" Rizka said.

"Crazier than usual, then." Entering the smithy, Big Franko tossed his medical box aside, picked up hammer and tongs, and banged away at the anvil for no particular purpose. "Pay me no mind," he said apologetically. "It's the Zipple."

Staying indoors gave no protection. The Zipple whispered through cracks and crevices, whimpered down chimneys, never ceasing. Housewives claimed the Zipple soured milk and addled eggs. The town clung to one hope: It would go away in a few weeks.

This summer, the Zipple seemed especially aggravating. Big Franko turned glum and silent, not at all his normal disposition. Mr. Mellish, more fidgety than ever, broke several strings on his zither. Miss Letta, needlewoman of perfection, found her stitches going crooked and, more than once, pricked her finger. Though joyously betrothed, the schoolmaster and the seamstress exchanged, for the first time, a few snippy words. Hatvan, drowsing at his table in Mr. Farkas's inn, would suddenly jump up and shout, "To arms! To arms!" Pugash shaved his customers so recklessly they feared loss of an earlobe.

In the streets, the mildest townsfolk berated and insulted one another. Fistfights broke out over trifles; Constable Shicker gave up trying to stop them. Someone maliciously flung a cobblestone through Mr. Sobako's window, and the outraged fishmonger stormed from his shop to belabor an innocent passerby with a salted codfish. The number of patients limping to Rizka's wagon grew larger, in a steady stream of blackened eyes, swollen jaws, bloody noses, and a rainbow of colorful bruises.

At the next council meeting, Sharpnack took action.

"The town is out of hand." The chief councilor always showed grim satisfaction in announcing bad news. "The situation—intolerable."

"It's the Zipple," said Mayor Pumpa.

"Zipple nonsense," retorted Sharpnack. "A pitiful excuse for misconduct, ruffianly behavior, for giving in to the baser instincts. Do you see me affected? Is my mind clouded? Not in the least. I ignore the Zipple and all the old wives' rubbish about it. The town has gotten out of control by sheer perversity and contrariness entirely on its own. We are teetering on the brink of disorder——"

"One thing I won't stand for is teetering," Podskalny put in. "It can wreak havoc on the cloth trade."

"What's this, hey?" General Hatvan blinked his eyes open. "Who's been teetering? Court-martial the rogue!"

"It begins with public slackness," Sharpnack went on. "Insults, rudeness, incivility. Where does it lead? To rampaging, rioting, flouting municipal authority. It must be nipped in the bud."

"I quite agree to nipping the teetering," said Mayor Pumpa. "But, Chief Councilor, how do you propose to keep people from insulting each other? They've been doing it for years."

"Make it illegal," said Sharpnack. "Simple as that. Pass a law against it and the matter's settled. The law's the law; the public will gladly obey it. They'll be grateful we're saving them from their own worst nature.

"I have taken on myself the burden of drafting such a measure." Sharpnack handed around a sheaf of papers. "It must be put into effect immediately."

Mayor Pumpa frowned at the closely written pages. "Good heavens, do you expect me to read all this?"

"Not necessary," Sharpnack assured him. "I can explain the essence of it. Citizens are henceforth forbidden to defame, slander, or otherwise offend each other. If convicted of this criminal misbehavior, they will suffer imprisonment——"

"Chief Councilor, there's a difficulty," Fibich raised a hand. "If you please, let me point out——"

"I don't please, and you'll point out nothing," retorted Sharpnack. "Hold your tongue."

"This really won't do at all." Mayor Pumpa had been scanning the document. "Trials? Convictions? I'm to judge them? Chief Councilor, you're piling work on me. I don't have time for that sort of thing."

"I must remind you," Fibich persisted. "Allow me to mention—"

"Not another word out of you!" Sharpnack focused his well-known glare on the town clerk. "Not a peep, not a whisper, you creeping rodent, or I'll squash you."

Fibich choked and bit his lips. Sharpnack turned to Mayor Pumpa. "Here's the beauty of it: There's no need for judicial thought. Everything is spelled out in detail, clear, straightforward, determined in advance. Offenses are listed, penalties already calculated. Whatever trials may be held, a jackass could conduct them. I shall handle the cases myself. Further, I predict: The impudent Gypsy will surely be the first one brought before the bar of justice, and I shall see that she is safely locked away indefinitely."

The council, at Sharpnack's urging, voted agreement and congratulated themselves on restoring tranquility to Greater Dunitsa. Mayor Pumpa read out the proclamation from the town hall balcony; relieved at settling an unruly state of affairs, he happily went home to his family.

Sharpnack's prediction was wrong. Next day, Constable Shicker arrested Mr. Karpath.

It began, as Rizka later found out, when the nautical carpenter returned a pair of boots Mr. Makkar had made for him.

"They pinch my toes." Karpath flung the boots onto the shoemaker's counter. "You botched your work. I can barely take a comfortable step. So keep them. Let's have my money back."

"Out of my shop!" Makkar snapped—he had been testy and grumpy all morning. "My boots? It's your feet. They must have swollen since I measured them. Money paid, money kept. Be glad anything fits you at all."

"Greedy swine, then see how they fit you!" Karpath, himself edgy and ill-tempered, tried to cram one of the offending boots over the shoemaker's head; in turn, Makkar swung his cobbler's last at the irate carpenter. Yelling, shoving, the two scuffled into the street. In moments, a crowd gathered, some trying to separate them, others merrily egging them on.

Luckily, Constable Shicker arrived before the combatants damaged one another. "What's all this?" he demanded as the onlookers pressed around him, eager to give their own account of what had happened.

"He called me a swine." Makkar gestured at the crowd. "They're my witnesses."

Constable Shicker looked unhappy. "Under the new law, that's a class one insult."

"The devil it is!" Karpath exclaimed. "If I'd meant to insult him, I'd have called him a pig. That's what you are, cobbler. A pig!"

"Ah, now you've gone and done it for sure." Constable Shicker sighed. He always felt morose at having to arrest anyone; it interfered with his day. "All right, Karpath, you just come along quietly."

Karpath showed no inclination to come along quietly or otherwise, but some of the bystanders aided Shicker in his duty by swarming over the outraged and muscular carpenter and finally succeeded in frog-marching him to the town hall.

Karpath, still struggling, was hauled to the same courtroom where the famous chicken trial had taken place. Now, however, Sharpnack sat on the bench, with Fibich beside him to note down the proceedings.

"All right, Constable." Sharpnack raised a dismissive hand before Shicker had finished his report. "Don't waste the court's time on details. I've heard enough." He riffled through his papers. "Pig, you say? That would be in the category of bestial epithets. The specified penalty—as chief prosecutor, I have the prerogative to increase it in the light of a flagrant violation, which this most certainly is.

"Since yours is the first case brought to my attention under the new ordinance, I mean to make an example of you, a severe one, to discourage future malefactors. You are sentenced to the municipal jail for a length of time that I authorize myself to determine later."

"Lock me up?" Karpath, ready to climb onto the bench,

had to be pulled back. "The Zipple's shriveled your brain! So I called the shoemaker a pig? You're a braying jackass!"

"That," Sharpnack declared, "will cost you an additional ten days."

"How much if I called you a numbskull?" Karpath shouted. "An addlepated lubber? A long-nosed lumphead? Do I get a special rate for quantity?"

"You'll get more than you ever bargained for." Sharpnack rapped his gavel. "Constable, take him away."

Fibich, meantime, had been tugging at Sharpnack's robe, while Sharpnack kept shaking him off like an annoying gadfly.

"But—but, Chief Councilor," Fibich blurted out. "The difficulty—I tried to tell you before. We don't have a jail."

Prisoners at the Bar

FROM THE LOOK on Sharpnack's face, Fibich might as well have told him the town had no horse trough. "What the devil are you jabbering about? Of course we have a jail."

"Yes, Chief Councilor, we do—in the technical sense," Fibich stammered. "But, well, it's rather full. You see—"

"Nonsense!" Sharpnack made a great effort not to lay hands on the clerk. "How can it be full? Are there prisoners in it? No, not a one."

Sharpnack, to that extent, was correct. Greater Dunitsa had never felt a need to find offenders worthy of being fed and lodged at the town's expense; and so the jail had indeed been empty for years. Fibich, on the other hand, was equally correct:

"Yes, Chief Councilor. No prisoners whatever. The difficulty, as I tried to explain—when you were convicted of
chicken stealing—I mean to say, when you ordered this
courtroom tidied up, we had to store the old clutter in the
jail. We've only the one cell, and now it's quite encumbered
with odds and ends."

"Am I to be badgered by administrative trivia?" Sharpnack
rolled up his eyes; the town clerk was twanging at his nerves.
"Clear out all that rubbish. See to it immediately."

"There's a lot," said Fibich. "It may take a while. Perhaps
Mr. Karpath should go away and come back another time."

"Oh, no. That's your problem, not mine." The carpenter
could be as knotty and cross-grained as his lumber. Having
ranted at being locked up, by sheer contrariness he now decided it was what he wanted more than anything else. "I've
been sentenced to jail, so to jail I'll go. It's my right as a law-
abiding citizen."

Sharpnack, glowering, turned to Constable Shicker. "Get
him out of here. Make room. I don't care how."

The town jail at the end of the corridor was the size of a
large closet, about as spacious as the bedchambers at Mr.
Farkas's inn. As Fibich warned, it was chockablock with ailing
furniture banished from the courtroom. Fibich had to go and
find the missing key; then he and Shicker evicted as many of
the occupants as possible at short notice. Karpath, nevertheless, had to be practically shoehorned inside. Fibich and the
constable shouldered shut the rusty iron grating.

"There. Satisfied?" Shicker said to Karpath, who had clambered atop a heap of torn straw mattresses. "You're officially incarceriated."

"When's dinner?" said Karpath.

The carpenter had never been much of a popular figure, so the townsfolk either ignored his arrest or decided it served him right. The only complaint came from Constable Shicker. A couple of days later, he sought an audience with Sharpnack.

"Here's the way of it, Chief Councilor," he began. "As you might say, it's like Mr. Farkas chasing cockroaches, if you take my meaning."

Sharpnack looked down his nose. "I am not familiar with the habits of disgusting insects."

"They scatter, is what they do," said Shicker. "Now, our townsfolk, you see, there's more of them than there is of me. They're ragging each other, carrying on worse than ever. But as soon as they get wind I'm in the vicinity, they run off; then another bang-up starts. Chief Councilor, I can't be everywhere at once. I'm not obsequious—"

"You mean ubiquitous," Fibich helpfully put in.

"That, too," said Shicker. "Keep an eye on the whole town by myself? No, if you want proper enforcement, sir, deputized assistance is required."

"Very well." Sharpnack nodded. "Round up a dozen or so stout fellows. Swear them in as deputies."

"It's not the swearing, it's the money," said Shicker. "They'll have to be recompsensed and renumerated. You'll find no-body to do this kind of hazardous duty for gratis."

The constable, Sharpnack admitted, had a strong point. In his capacity as treasurer, he grudgingly authorized the necessary funds. For his part, Constable Shicker hired the town's most notorious brawlers and troublemakers, calculating if they worked for him he would avoid having to arrest them.

Sharpnack was pleased at the result. He refused to pay for uniforms, but this turned out to be an advantage. The towns-folk had no sure idea who the deputies were or when one might suddenly appear out of nowhere. Greater Dunitsa had never been quieter.

"Too quiet to suit me," Rizka later said to Big Franko, who had come to repair an axle on her wagon. "I liked it better when they squabbled now and again. Instead, they're always looking over their shoulders as if they had a crick in the neck."

"Don't worry," the blacksmith gloomily said. "It won't last. Nothing does. Besides, what can you do about it?"

"I'll think it over," said Rizka.

Big Franko, as things turned out, was right. That same day, Mr. Karras, the musical corn dealer, brought his dog into the barber shop already filled with waiting clients.

"Remove that canine." Pugash, in the process of shaving Mr. Chudra the baker, found his hand trembling more than usual. "He makes me twitch, the way he sits there licking his chops."

"That's right," agreed Mr. Chudra, having suffered a few slices from the barber's reckless razor. "What, he's waiting for some part of me to drop on the floor?"

"Of course he isn't," Mr. Karras protested. "He's had his breakfast. Besides, he always comes with me. You know that, Pugash."

"Well, he comes here no more," Pugash declared. "Take that dandruff-ridden mutt outside. Scrofulous hound! He's a disgrace to my tonsorial parlor."

"You mind what you're saying." Mr. Karras, usually a harmonious, lyrical soul, jumped to his feet. "Insult my dog, you insult me!"

"Take yourself outside as well!" Pushed to the limits of his patience which had, since the arrival of the Zipple, daily grown shorter, Pugash flung his shaving basin at the dog, missed his mark, and drenched Mr. Karras.

As luck would have it, with the clients milling around, Mr. Chudra trying to escape from the barber chair, Mr. Karras spitting out soap bubbles, the dog yelping and leaping, and Pugash threatening to dock the creature's tail and his master's ears, a pair of Shicker's deputies materialized on the scene and the indignant barber was hauled away.

Worse yet lay in store. General Hatvan, happening to emerge from the inn and seeing Pugash struggling in the clutches of the law, ran up and pulled out his saber.

"Unhand him! That's an order! Hup, hup!" shouted Hatvan. "Arrest my second in command? How dare you! Scurvy idiots! Defaulting malingerers!"

The deputies exchanged glances. "I don't know what *malingerers* is," one said, "but *scurvy idiots* should be enough." With several more deputies hurrying to assist their colleagues, Hatvan and Pugash were jostled into the courtroom. Sharpnack, taken aback, stared in dismay at the prisoners before him.

"Barber Pugash," he said, after hearing the charges, "I am shocked and appalled by your conduct. You, in full knowledge of the law, deliberately violated it."

"A dog!" Pugash, in fury, tore at his side whiskers. "I only insulted a dog!"

"The court does not differentiate." Sharpnack fixed a cold eye on the accused. If he had been at all tempted to dismiss the case, the temptation lasted no more than the fraction of a second. Sharpnack had a long memory. He vividly recalled gulping down the barber's mustard liniment, and it was not without satisfaction that he ordered Pugash locked up.

"And you, General." Sharpnack sighed heavily. "It grieves me deeply and personally to see you in these distressing circumstances. But you, a military man, appreciate the value of discipline and understand that no exception to the law can be made.

"Though I regret my judicial obligation, I count on you to

face your sentence with the courage of the valiant soldier that you are. Your fortitude and patience in suffering confinement will be an inspiration to us all."

"Inspiration, hey?" Hatvan went red as a turkey cock. "I'll have your guts for garters once I'm out!"

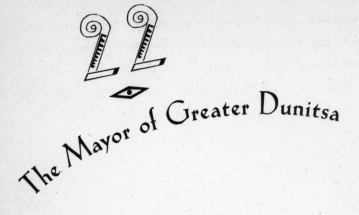

22

The Mayor of Greater Dunitsa

THE COURT CHOOSES to ignore that response," said Sharpnack. "Indeed, it makes a generous concession: As an ßofficer and a gentleman, you will be allowed to keep your saber. I accept your word of honor you will make no attempt to use it."

Fibich, drowning in paperwork, had not yet got around to clearing the cell; so, Hatvan and Pugash, grinding their teeth and cursing Sharpnack, were squeezed in with Mr. Karpath.

The cramped quarters grew still more cramped when, in the course of the day, several unlucky townsfolk were squashed inside. With Pugash loudly demanding mustache wax and a clean shirt, the general and carpenter berating each other, the new inmates protesting they had been arrested by mistake and yelling to be set loose, Fibich decided further housekeeping was risky. He threw up his hands in despair and left the prisoners to sort things out for themselves.

He did raise the subject next morning at the council meeting, where Hatvan's chair, like the saddle of a fallen warrior, was forlornly empty.

"They've been making a terrible racket," Fibich reported. "Perhaps if we declared an amnesty and sent them all home?"

"Sentences will be served; the law must take its course." Sharpnack had arrived late, puffy-eyed and pasty-faced. The Zipple has been unceasing, the little wind boring into his head like an earwig. He had tried counting sheep, then found himself counting prisoners. The usually attentive Mrs. Slatka had scorched his breakfast gruel; his pigeons flapped nervously in their loft; on his way to the town hall, he had been hooted at by a crowd of citizens, which obliged him to call for Constable Shicker and a few deputies as an escort. Shaken, he insisted on these officers staying with him in the council chamber to conduct him safely back home.

"Our right-thinking, civic-minded townspeople will realize we have acted for their own good." Sharpnack fidgeted with his papers. "They will be grateful to us."

"Us? What us?" burst out Podskalny, who likewise had not enjoyed a wink of sleep. "It was your idea, not mine. And I can tell you I haven't been thanked. On the contrary. Two of my best customers got locked up. They're thanking me? You listen here, Sharpnack. If the cloth trade falls off, you're the one to blame." Podskalny heaved around and shook a finger at the mayor. "You, too, Pumpa, with all your blather about nipping and teetering."

"Me? You were the first to come out against teetering," snapped Mayor Pumpa, whose own breakfast had been less than appetizing, and the kittens had upset his pitcher of milk. "Maundering about your cloth trade—rag trade, more like it. And mind what you're doing with that finger or I'll deal with you the way I did—"

"You deal with me? I'll deal with you!" cried Podskalny. "Bloated bumbler with a lump of moldy cheese for a brain! You're a waffling dunderhead and always were!"

"And you're a dyed-in-the-wool idiot, you pushcart peddler! You beached whale! You puffing blowfish!"

"Constable Shicker!" Sharpnack jumped to his feet. "Arrest these two gentlemen."

Mayor Pumpa and Mr. Podskalny, on the verge of trading blows as well as insults, spun around to unite in fury at the chief councilor.

"Have you gone mad?" bellowed Mayor Pumpa. "You mealy-mouthed nitwit, you can't arrest me. I'm a public official."

"You mimping, meeching, cretinous fool!" Podskalny's wattles vibrated. "Squint-eyed scarecrow! Snaggle-toothed spindleshanks! Do you forget who I am?"

"No one is above the law," declared Sharpnack, as the constable ruefully signaled his deputies to obey the chief councilor's orders. "What would be our reputation among the citizenry if we showed favoritism? You are performing a public service by demonstrating our complete impartiality. It is your civic duty to go to jail."

Mr. Podskalny and the mayor had to be shoved from behind to cram them into the cell. The current inmates, who now considered themselves old hands and seasoned convicts, greeted them with catcalls and whistles and ragged the two additions as mercilessly as if they were new boys at school.

In the council chamber, Fibich rocked his head in his hands, murmuring, "Dear me, good heavens, who'd have imagined!"

Sharpnack sat reflectively at the table, warmed by the satisfaction of having behaved righteously in accordance with his conscience and the law, which he considered to be identical.

"It occurs to me," he said to Fibich, who was still holding his head, "I must now assume the responsibilities of chief magistrate. I do so with a heavy heart, but with the firm resolution to serve honorably in that capacity until Mayor Pumpa returns.

"By the way, Fibich," he added, "where does he keep his chain of office?"

Sofiya Pumpa was in tears when she came to Rizka's wagon. "My father's in jail," she sobbed. "We went to see him. It's terrible. He's very unhappy; he's not used to being a criminal."

"We'll find a way to get him out." Rizka had already heard

the shocking news, but events had moved so quickly she had no time to give them her best thought. The sight of her weeping apprentice spurred her to immediate action.

"I want you to run a couple of errands for me," Rizka said, after turning the matter back and forth in her mind for a while. "I'll take care of the rest."

Sniffling but comforted when she heard what Rizka proposed, Sofiya hurried back to town. Rizka draped Petzel over her shoulder and sauntered down to the river.

There, as expected, she found Bagrat and the chicken brigade splashing in the water or sunning themselves on the bank. With the summer heat and ever-present Zipple, the urchins had lost interest in Sharpnack. But when Rizka explained her need for their services, they dutifully answered the call to arms and capered after her.

Rizka's calculations were excellent. Escorted by Constable Shicker and his deputies, Sharpnack had just come out of the town hall. The mayor's silver chain hung from his neck; an air of high purpose illuminated his lean features as he paced solemnly homeward for lunch.

Rizka glanced around. Sofiya, near the portals of the town hall, nodded and winked at her. Big Franko, her reserve force, stood alert in front of the inn. The chicken brigade awaited her orders.

"Charge!" she commanded.

Half of the chicken brigade ran to outflank Sharpnack; the rest engaged him from the rear, clucking and squawking, pumping their elbows up and down, putting thumbs in their ears and waggling their fingers. The deputies, taken by surprise, tried to capture the raiders. However, as Constable Shicker would have said, it was like chasing cockroaches. No sooner did an officer try to collar one of the urchins than three or four others diverted him. The brigade scattered, ducked away, and renewed the attack.

Sharpnack's face went livid. He shook his fists, roared at his assailants, but found no way to turn without being chivied and harassed from all sides. The onlookers and passersby made matters only worse, getting underfoot, hampering the officers, sometimes gleefully tripping them up.

A gap had opened in the circle of urchins. Seizing his best chance for escape, Sharpnack darted through the breach. He hiked up his robe and ran for dear life into the open square.

Rizka, like a shrewd field commander, judged this was the moment for her to join the fray. Petzel sprang from her shoulder and streaked beside her as she signaled the brigade to follow. With Rizka at his heels, and about to be hemmed in by the urchins, Sharpnack found his only clear path in the direction of the horse trough.

Whether Sharpnack meant to dodge around or vault over it would never be known, for Petzel, that instant, scurried between the chief councilor's legs. Sharpnack, in mid-stride, stumbled, lurched forward; leaping into the air, arms outspread as if he were about to fly, he pitched headfirst into the horse trough. Sharpnack's upper half vanished underwater;

the remainder kicked and flailed. By the time he managed to surface and sit up, with his knees bent over the edge of the trough, Rizka had begun a chicken-style war dance, flapping her arms and crowing at the top of her voice.

Sharpnack's lank hair was plastered like seaweed around his head. Snorting, spitting water, he turned his full fury on Rizka. "You!" he bawled. "You're the ringleader in this! Misbegotten mongrel! Lice-ridden guttersnipe!"

"Here now, this won't do." Constable Shicker arrived at the horse trough. Sofiya, at Rizka's instruction, had warned him to expect a commotion. "All respect, Your Honor, those were straight out insults. Begging your pardon, but you're under arrest."

"She's nothing but a Gypsy," sputtered Sharpnack as the deputies hauled him out, soaked to the skin. "Fool! You can't arrest me!"

Shicker clapped a beefy hand on the chief councilor's shoulder. "I don't know if being a Gypsy counts one way or the other. We'll have to let the judge settle that."

"I'm the judge!" Sharpnack tried to squirm free of Shicker's grasp. "I dismiss the case!"

With Sharpnack dripping and raging, and Shicker warning him not to make matters worse for himself, Big Franko strolled up. Rizka grinned at him:

"I figured he'd insult somebody. Probably me."

Marched into the courtroom, Sharpnack exploded again.

On the bench, peering from behind stacks of books and papers, sat Fibich.

"Get down from there, you goggle-eyed polecat!" bawled Sharpnack. "You're no judge, you slinking rodent!"

"I'm the only one available," Fibich apologetically replied. "But we'll make do. As you said, any jackass can deal with these cases. Also, it saves you the trouble of having to sentence yourself."

"You haven't heard the last of this, Gypsy maggot!" Sharpnack flung at Rizka. "I'm not done with you. Turn justice upside down? I'll teach you what justice is!"

"I'll be glad to know," said Rizka. "We'll talk about it after Judge Fibich lets you out of jail."

"I'm sorry the jail's rather full," said Fibich, "but if you just hunch up and pull in your stomach a little, you'll have room.

"Forgive me for mentioning it, Chief Councilor," he added. "I'm afraid I'll have to take that silver chain from you."

The new convict was welcomed with even louder hoots and jeers than Podskalny and Mayor Pumpa received. In the cell, filled to bursting, the fuming chief councilor had to flatten himself against the grating, his long nose between the bars, with Hatvan's knees jabbing the small of his back.

"Congratulations, Fibich," Rizka said. "You were a fine judge. Now, for the rest of my plan: While Pumpa's in jail, you'll be mayor. Then—"

"But I can't. No, no, simply not possible. Nor legal." Fibich pulled off his spectacles and polished them nervously. "Sofiya brought your message, but I wasn't able to explain. I can't be mayor, you see, because I don't count as being in line for it."

"You have to," Rizka insisted. "Or else everything goes wrong."

"I've studied it all out in the town charter," Fibich pressed on. "There's a way around it. In the circumstances—an emergency, which this certainly is—I'm allowed to appoint a temporary mayor."

"Good," said Rizka. "Here's Big Franko. He's just the right one for the job."

"Not me," said the blacksmith. "I'd rather tend a constipated horse; it's a cleaner business."

"Since it's up to me to decide," Fibich put in, "what I had in mind from the beginning: My dear girl, I officially appoint—you."

Big Franko slapped his leg and broke out laughing. "Caught in your own scheme! You're stuck with it, *chiriklo*. Or I should say: Mayor Rizka."

The Chiriklos

"OH, NO, YOU DON'T," said Rizka. "I have better ways to spend my time." She glanced from Big Franko to Fibich and back again. Rizka knew when she was outnumbered and outvoted. "All right, all right," she said. "If that's how it is, let's get the business over with.

"First thing," Rizka declared, "I officially repeal Sharpnack's law. Second thing: Fibich, go let out the prisoners. They're all pardoned, even Sharpnack. Hatvan and Podskalny can be councilors—"

"What?" exclaimed Big Franko. "Sharpnack and the whole crew of idiots back again?"

"Better the idiots we know than idiots we don't know. I can handle them," said Rizka. "Last thing: I resign. In favor of

Mayor Pumpa. Give him his chain and tell him he should thank Sofiya—"

Rizka paused. "Do you notice anything different?"

"No." Big Franko cocked his head. "Wait, yes, now I do."

"Right," said Rizka. "The Zipple just stopped."

"At last!" Fibich heaved a sigh of relief. "Goodness me, I'd begun to think it would never go away. A blessing! Now, finally, everything will calm down."

"I wouldn't go quite that far," said Rizka.

Satisfied she had done enough of a good day's work, with as much civic duty as she could swallow all at once, Rizka slept solidly that night, slept, in fact, later than usual. What roused her was Petzel chirping and trilling. She opened the wagon door to see the cat stretched full length on the step, his ears alert and long tail twitching.

A dozen or more slim, black and white birds strutted around the clearing or perched in the trees. Petzel eyed them intently but made no attempt to pounce.

"*Chiriklos!*" Rizka caught her breath. "Petzel, if they're here, the Gypsies aren't far behind."

She hurried down one of the forest tracks, hoping for a glimpse of a caravan on the way. Finding none, she turned and ran in the other direction, pressing deeper into the woods. She saw no trace of campfires or wheel ruts. By the time she got back to her *vardo*, Sofiya was waiting.

"Look at them all," Rizka's apprentice demon called out. "I've never seen birds like that."

After her teacher explained the omen, the delighted Sofiya took for granted that Rizka's Gypsies were hers as well. "I can't wait to see them. When are they coming?"

"Soon." Rizka kept her gaze on the fringe of trees.

"Will your father be with them?"

"Why else would they come here?" Rizka said.

"Will he take you away? If he does, I'll go, too," declared Sofiya. When Rizka did not answer, she considered the matter settled and pressed on. "Oh—I have to tell you. I sneaked into the passage behind the council chamber wall. I wish you'd been there.

"When Sharpnack came in, they all started yelling at him—all but little Mr. Fibich; he just kept polishing his spectacles. Mr. Podskalny got so red in the face I thought he'd burst. He said Sharpnack nearly ruined the cloth business and should have stayed in jail. The names my father called him"—Sofiya giggled—"I'm not supposed to know what they mean.

"General Hatvan was jumping up and down, he even pulled out his saber and challenged Sharpnack to a duel. But Sharpnack only rolled his eyes up at the ceiling and talked about his sacred responsibility and doing his duty. The way he droned on, he'd have put them to sleep if they hadn't been so mad at him.

"They wanted to vote something bad they could do to

Sharpnack, but they couldn't agree on what would be bad enough. I don't think they'll ever make up their minds. Let's go watch."

Rizka shook her head. "I'll wait for the caravan."

"I want to see it, too."

"You will. Promise."

Sofiya went back to the town hall. Rizka sat down beside Petzel.

"He'll find me," she said. "Where we'll go then, I don't know. One thing sure: You'll be with me. Always."

She stayed there all day. At dusk, she lit a lamp and put it in the window of the *vardo*. There was no caravan.

She gave up her usual rounds and errands. For several days, she paced the clearing or perched on the steps of the wagon. The leaves were beginning to turn. The woodland smelled of damp earth; mist hung over the ground. The *chiriklos* had flown off; one day they were whistling and chattering; the next, gone.

From time to time, Sofiya would come to wait with her. Late one morning, while Sofiya was playing with Petzel, Rizka heard the creak of wagon wheels and the jingle of harness. She held her breath, listening closely.

She jumped to her feet. A *vardo* rolled out of the mist.

The driver tossed aside the reins and swung down from the wagon. Rizka started toward him. The man was tall, rawboned, with a great eagle's beak of a nose. A wide-brimmed hat, as battered as Rizka's, sat rakishly on the side of his head; gold chains glittered at his neck. He halted as Rizka approached and looked her up and down. His weather-blackened face was seamed and crisscrossed with lines of laughter and hard living.

"Well, now. Little Rizka." The big *rom* hooked his thumbs into the red sash at his waist. "You're taller than I thought."

Rizka stared at him. With loose, easy strides, the man went to her wagon as if he owned it and glanced inside.

"Neatly kept. You sleep there? Yes, that's your mother's blood in you. A true *rom* sleeps outside, on the ground. Who wants a roof?

"Strong girl," he added with approval. "You could pass for a *rom*. You're alone? Not good. We all live as best we can, but you'll be better off with your *pralos*—your brethren."

Rizka's chin went up. "Who are you?"

"Leric. I'm the *barossan*—leader of the caravan"—he gestured toward the clearing where two more wagons halted—"my *kumpania*. I have news of your father."

Rizka studied him intently. Gypsies were clambering from the *vardo*s. Some dozen youngsters had begun unhitching the horses and gathering kindling for cookfires. They dressed much like their elders: the boys in mended jackets and breeches, the girls in bright, swirling skirts, gold loops in their ears and bracelets covering their thin arms.

"Leric?" Rizka set her eyes squarely on the *barossan*. "Is that really your name? Tell me the truth."

"Does one *rom* lie to another?"

Rizka lowered her gaze. "I thought, for a moment—"

"I know what you thought. I was afraid you might. No. I'm not your father. He—Janos—rode with me some while. We were close as brothers. What do you remember of him?"

"He was tall. He played the fiddle. That's mostly all I know."

"Yes. Well, he told me everything about you. A tiny girl then. You were all his heart. He loved you."

"Loved?" Rizka burst out. "Why did he leave?"

Leric put his hands on Rizka's shoulders. "Understand. Your father was a good man. But we *rom* are children of the wind. We stay nowhere; we go everywhere. He, too, followed the wind. When it called him, he answered. He had to. It was in his blood and bone. Forgive him."

"For being himself?" Rizka turned away. She said flatly, "He's dead, isn't he?"

Leric nodded. "Fever. Some winters ago. It wiped out most of the *kumpania*. He would have come for you, one day or another. He meant to. He wanted to. You were in his mind to the end. I promised him I'd look after you. Our road has been long, with many turnings; but, at last, it brought us here."

Rizka did not answer. She went abruptly into the *vardo* and sat stroking Petzel on her lap. Sofiya popped her head through the door:

"You should see! They've got cookpots, and tables, and stools, and some chickens, and the wagons all around. It's almost like Greater Dunitsa. Are they going to live here?"

"They won't stay long," Rizka said. "They never do. Go home, little one."

The Caravan

SHE SAT IN the *vardo* the rest of the day. Leric and his *kumpania* did her the kindness of leaving her to herself. At nightfall, the *rom* gathered around the campfire. Someone began playing a fiddle. She knew the melody. She had always known it. As if it were her father's voice, she once had told Big Franko. She had believed it whispered he would come back for her and never leave again. Now, listening, she understood he was sadly, tenderly, saying good-bye. She had waited; there was no one to wait for. Only then did she cry, which she did not want to do. At some point, a woman came in. Saying nothing, she stroked Rizka's hair and rocked her back and forth like a child. Rizka finally went to sleep in the comforting arms of a stranger.

At daybreak, the *rom* were up and busy. The woman who had come to her—Melitza, the *barossan*'s wife—led Rizka from the wagon and sat her down with the *kumpania* at their morning meal. Melitza, as generously proportioned as Mrs. Pumpa, offered her a tin plate. Rizka shook her head.

"Take it," Melitza said gently. "If you're going to be a *rom*, the first thing you need to learn: When there's food, you eat it. Now. Maybe it won't be here tomorrow."

Leric put an arm around Rizka's shoulders. "You'll be fine. Things don't look so bad after your belly's full. You'll cheer up once you're on the road." The *barossan*'s face wrinkled into a huge grin. "You've been too close to folk who live in houses. A roof over their heads cuts off the air and softens their brains. Ah, these *gorgios*—that's anyone who isn't a *rom*—you have to feel sorry for the poor devils. Half of them are crazy; the other half are lunatics. Still, I guess you managed well enough. How you put up with them, I'll never know."

"Easy. Just a little nudge here and there." Rizka, finishing her plate, began to brighten. Leric's good humor was contagious, and, after all, she was Rizka. She soon began telling about the chicken trial, the ghost in the town hall, Sharpnack's nose, and General Hatvan with herrings stuffed into his pants.

Leric threw back his head and laughed. "You've got your wits about you. You'll make a first-class *rom* and even teach us a trick or two. We'll teach you a few things, as well. Do you know how to catch fish without a hook? Read our secret trail markings? Talk to horses?

"Speaking of horses," Leric added, "you'll need one to pull your *vardo*. We'll want a string of remounts, too. Strong ones, not broken-winded old nags."

"I have a friend," Rizka said. "I'll take you to him. He'll get them for you."

"Good." Leric nodded. "We have to head south before the weather starts to bite. The *pralos* can go into town and raise a bit of cash: pots and pans to mend, scissors to sharpen. A little fortune-telling—Melitza's clever at it—as if we could tell anyone's fortunes, least of all our own. But the *gorgios* expect it. See a *rom*, they either start feeling their pockets or want their palms read. Where's the harm if it makes them happy? So, let's get about our business."

"Keep clear of town," Rizka warned. "Don't go there. You'll run into trouble with Sharpnack, for one."

"That's right," piped up Sofiya, who had hurried back to camp and squatted beside Rizka in time to hear this last of the conversation. "I came to tell you. As soon as they got wind of Gypsies in the neighborhood, the council had a meeting. I listened. They'd almost agreed how to punish Sharpnack, but he kept changing the subject, carrying on about the Gypsies. They ought to be chased away, he said. He called them a pack of thieves and villains. Nobody in town should have anything to do with them. He even wanted all the children locked indoors so the Gypsies couldn't steal them." She turned to Leric and asked hopefully, "Is that what you do?"

"We haven't enough of our own? We should steal more?"

The *barossan* snorted and tapped the side of his head. "*Gorgios!* Crazy, like I said. Thieves and villains? That depends whether you're inside looking out or outside looking in. There's as many thieves living in houses as riding in *vardos*, glad to pick your pockets and swear you'll be all the better for it. Ach, enough about *gorgios*. Horses first."

Leaving Sofiya chattering with the youngsters, Rizka took Leric to Big Franko's forge, keeping to the back streets and alleys as a matter of caution. The blacksmith put aside his work to greet the *barossan*.

"She's right," Big Franko said, when Rizka told him what Leric had planned. "Don't let your people set foot in town. Too dangerous. Sharpnack's been trying to stir folk against you—as if you Gypsies had horns and a tail."

"We do," said Leric. "I left mine in the wagon."

The blacksmith laughed good-naturedly and motioned toward the stable behind the shop. "I have a few decent mounts. Not the best, not the worst, but they'll do well for you. We'll dicker a fair price."

As Leric went to inspect the horses, Big Franko hung back a moment with Rizka. "What's amiss, little bird? There's something. I can see it."

The blacksmith listened quietly while Rizka told the news that Leric had brought. He put an arm around her shoulders. "I'm sorry. It's not how I expected things would turn out for you. I thought—I'm not sure what I thought."

Big Franko said no more for a long moment. When he

spoke again, his voice was heavy. "So. What now, *chiriklo*? You'll fly off? I always knew it might happen."

"Yes. You did." From one of her pockets Rizka took out the small iron bird. "And you gave me this. For luck. Do you think I'd forgotten?"

"I hoped not."

Rizka touched Big Franko's battered hand. "I'll always remember. Everything. Even the time I bit you.

"Leric and his *kumpania*"—she hesitated a little—"he says I'll be better off with them. He doesn't have a high opinion of *gorgios*."

"Sometimes neither do I." Big Franko held up his palms as if they were the pans of a scale. "*Gorgios*? Gypsies? At the end, it comes to the same. No one's as bad as they seem—or as good as they think they are. You'll do whatever's best."

"When don't I?" Rizka said.

Sofiya Leads an Invasion

SOFIYA HAD LEFT by the time Rizka, Leric, and Big Franko led the horses to the camp. The *rom* were mending their gear and repairing their *vardos*; though pinched for money and supplies, Leric planned for the *kumpania* to start south before the end of the week.

Big Franko stayed to watch while the Gypsy craftsmen hammered out bridle bits and fitted iron rims to wagon wheels. "You fellows know tricks of the trade I've never seen," he admitted to Leric. "I'll have to learn—"

He stopped as Rizka raised a warning hand. From the direction of the town came a murmur of voices and what sounded like an army crashing through the underbrush.

Fearing a mob was on the way to drive them out or burn

down the camp, Leric shouted for the *rom* to stand ready to defend themselves. Moments later, the first invader dashed into the clearing and headed straight for Rizka.

It was Sofiya.

"They're here!" The girl's pigtails seemed to keep flying even after she halted.

"They? Who?" Rizka took Sofiya by the shoulders and tried to stop her from bouncing up and down.

"Sharpnack didn't want Gypsies in town? So, here's the town come to the Gypsies! It was my idea; I thought of it," Sofiya crowed—Rizka had neglected to teach her student to be modest about her accomplishments—"I brought them, as many as I could. That's what you'd have done, isn't it?"

"Little one," said Rizka, as Sofiya pranced back and forth, "you're getting to be as big a trickster as I am."

Meantime, Bagrat and the chicken brigade had run into the clearing, fanning out through the camp, gaping in wonder at the colorful *vardos*, and chattering with the Gypsy youngsters. A crowd of townsfolk followed. Some carried pots and pans to be mended; others were simply curious, especially since Sharpnack had forbidden them to be there.

Seeing themselves overrun not by invaders but by possible customers, the women of the caravan lost no time in spreading out blankets or setting up tables covered with bits of jewelry, gold chains, strings of bright beads, belts, and kerchiefs. As Rizka watched in astonishment, the camp began looking like a market square and town holiday combined.

While the chicken brigade struck up an instant friendship with the Gypsy lads, finding them comrades-in-arms and brothers under the skin, the townsfolk eagerly bought all the finery they could, paying in coins or bartering sacks of flour, baskets of vegetables, and strings of sausages.

To her further surprise, Rizka caught sight of Mayor and Mrs. Pumpa, with the adorable twins and little Roswitha wide-eyed at the hustle and bustle. At the same time, she glimpsed Mellish and Miss Letta and squeezed her way through the press of townsfolk to join them.

"I'm glad you're here," said Rizka. "So, you've come to see the Gypsies, too."

"Not entirely," said the schoolmaster. "All quite interesting, yes, from an ethnological and folkloric point of view. An excellent opportunity to observe their manners and customs. But—no, more than anything we've come for your sake. So has half the town, it would appear."

"Sofiya's been telling everyone you intend to depart with them," said Miss Letta, drawing Rizka aside. "I wished to speak with you before that event takes place.

"To express my thanks to you, for one thing," the seamstress went on, making sure the schoolmaster's attention had drifted toward the Gypsies. Miss Letta lowered her voice. "And for another, to confide in you regarding the present relationship between myself and my dear Mr. Mellish. Ever since you helped him with his balloon, he has not been quite the same."

"I'm sorry. I never meant——"

"No, no, his change has been most exciting," Miss Letta said. "The balloon flight seems to have galvanized his spirits. It was never his habit to advance rapidly and I feared our engagement would be long and possibly endless.

"But now," the seamstress continued, "he has become definitely assertive—in his own genteel way, of course. He has insisted with surprising firmness on my naming a wedding date at the soonest possible moment."

"Wonderful!" exclaimed Rizka. "He really has advanced."

Miss Letta gave a neatly folded sigh. "In gratitude for your assistance, I had hoped you would attend the ceremony as my maid of honor. Alas, you will not be here to grace the joyful occasion."

Before Rizka could answer, someone pulled at her sleeve. Esperanza Podskalny (née Pumpa) motioned for her to step a little away from the crowd and spoke quickly in Rizka's ear:

"While you're still here, there's something we want to tell you," she whispered, as Lorins proudly twirled his mustache which, for reasons of its own, had grown more luxurious since the wedding. "We're looking forward to the arrival of a new Podskalny. That is, half a Podskalny and half a Pumpa."

"We haven't told our parents yet," Lorins added. "We wanted you to be the first to know."

"With a baby on the way, our fathers might stop squabbling. Or at least have something to argue about instead of cheese and rags," Esperanza said. "And you, for all you've done to help us, we'd have liked you to be the godmother."

Rizka barely had time to congratulate the happy couple. One of the *rom* had brought out a fiddle and launched into a wild *csardas*, which set the onlookers stamping their feet. On Mayor Pumpa's lap, little Roswitha clapped her chubby hands in time to the music, and some of the townsfolk ventured to dance, not only with one another, but as well to kick up their heels with the Gypsies. More newcomers arrived, among them Fibich, as enraptured by the *vardos* and whirling dancers as he had been by Ali Baba's cave.

"Ah, there you are, dear girl," he called out, making his way toward Rizka. "I didn't want to miss seeing you before you left. I won't have much chance to get away from my office—after what the council did to me."

"Don't tell me you got yourself in trouble." Rizka frowned with concern.

"Not exactly. Well, you see, they finally decided how to punish Sharpnack."

"So then?"

"So they gave me extra duties—"

"What?" cried Rizka. "That's a punishment for Sharpnack?"

"Oh, yes. He was furious, fit to be tied, quite beside himself. I've never seen him so vexed. As I was saying, I'll keep on being town clerk, notary, all the rest—"

"I don't understand."

"What they did," said Fibich, "on top of my other duties— well, what they did: They elected me chief councilor."

"Fibich, that's absolutely delicious." Rizka clapped her hands. "Perfect! And Sharpnack's out of a job."

"No," said Fibich. "He'll be my assistant clerk."

"Better and better! There's a real comedown for him. Serves him right."

"Actually, I'll be glad for the help," said Fibich, "I'm so far behind in my work. I'll keep him busy, indeed I will. I'll have him start inspecting sewers and cesspools. Also, he'll be Commissioner of Rodent Abatement—"

"In other words," Rizka put in, "he's the town's official rat-catcher."

"Yes," Fibich said, "but if he does well and shows promise, he could eventually move up to issuing dog licenses."

"Fibich, come here," said Rizka, wiping tears of laughter from her eyes. "I never thought I'd get to kiss a chief councilor." She suited the action to her words by planting a couple of delighted kisses on his blushing cheeks.

"Let's find Big Franko and tell him the news." With Fibich behind her, Rizka started toward the wagon where she last had seen the blacksmith. She had to pause at every step, continually greeted by townsfolk who never before had spoken to her. Karpath had left his lumberyard for the occasion. The nautical carpenter beckoned to her.

"I wanted to tell you," he whispered. "I've made new calculations. There's bound to be another flood sooner or later. This time, the big one. Aye, lass, a real monster. What a shame you'll miss it."

Fibich had vanished into the crowd. She turned back to find him when the fiddler abruptly stopped playing. The dancers halted in mid-measure. The chicken brigade left off romping with the Gypsy youngsters. The laughter withered away. The onlookers fell glum and silent, as if each suddenly recalled a bad case of indigestion, a toothache, an old love affair gone wrong, unpaid bills, broken promises, and childhood miseries until now forgotten.

Sharpnack stood in the clearing.

Rizka Goes Home

"CAN I BELIEVE MY EYES? Shocking! Appalling!"
The arrival of Sharpnack had draped a clammy black shroud
over the merrymakers. Daylight faded; even the sun began
escaping as rapidly as possible. "Citizens of Greater Dunitsa
cavorting with dissolute riffraff! Have you lost all sense of
decency?"

Mayor Pumpa pulled up his collar and jammed his hat over
his eyes, hoping to make himself invisible. He did not suc-
ceed. Sharpnack stabbed a finger at him:

"And you, Pumpa, who should set an example of municipal
virtue and high-mindedness! Permitting your wife and innocent offspring to witness this vulgar spectacle!"

Little Roswitha started bawling as if Sharpnack's presence

had brought on a gas bubble. The adorable twins clapped their hands over their ears and burrowed their faces in Mrs. Pumpa's sheltering bosom.

"Who invited you?" Rizka strode through the crowd and halted in front of Sharpnack. "This is none of your business."

"Nor yours." Sharpnack folded his arms and stared down his nose. His cheeks twitched and he grimaced as if he were about to pass a kidney stone. "You've played your last trick here, you corroding influence on right-thinking citizens. You're finally where you belong: in the midst of your own kind. Never will I have to lay eyes on you again."

"That's none of your doing," retorted Rizka. "I go where I please."

"Then go! The farther the better. Good riddance, I say. Good riddance to bad rubbish." Sharpnack motioned to Constable Shicker, standing uncomfortably behind him. "Do your duty. Disperse this riotous mob."

"If I were you, Shicker," put in Rizka, "I wouldn't try dispersing anything."

Caught between Sharpnack's glare and Rizka's advice, the constable rubbed his face and shifted from one foot to the other. Meantime, the onlookers had come to gather around Rizka.

"She's right, Shicker," someone called. "You just keep out of this."

"You, too, Sharpnack," another added. "Shove off. Make yourself useful. Go chase a few rats."

More townsfolk joined in with some colorful suggestions

of their own. The rest began hooting, jeering, and whistling through their teeth. Sharpnack, livid, gaped like one of Mr. Sobako's codfish.

"To your homes, all of you!" he commanded when he found his voice. "Begone from this den of iniquity!"

Someone, probably Bagrat, lobbed a mudball, which went flying past Sharpnack's ear. The crowd guffawed as he dodged the missile and nearly tumbled into the bushes. Constable Shicker, seeing which way the wind was blowing, hunched up his shoulders and tiptoed away. A few more clods were launched; the spectators moved closer.

"I refuse to dignify this disorderly assemblage with my presence." Sharpnack, observing how the distance between himself and his audience was growing rapidly smaller, took a backward step. "I'll waste no more of my valuable time."

He turned on his heel. His pace, which had begun with proper solemnity, quickened as the crowd pressed after him. His deliberate gait soon became a brisk trot, then a long-legged run as the townsfolk followed, whooping and squawking at his heels.

Sharpnack's pursuers surged past Rizka. Those who might have wanted to linger found themselves swept along with the crowd. Rizka glanced around at the deserted clearing.

Big Franko had come quietly beside her. "What's wrong? You don't look too happy."

"I wanted to give that long-nosed praying mantis a good piece of my mind. For a going-away present."

"He's not your concern anymore," Big Franko said. "You should be pleased. Everyone here was on your side. All in all, thanks to your friends, it's been a good day."

"Better than good. Profitable." Leric joined them. The *barossan* was filling a sack with coins. "More than we've taken in since we've been on the road."

"You'll do still better," Rizka told him, as they walked to the *vardo*. "Sharpnack can't stop anyone coming, no matter how he jaws at them. They had too good a time. They'll be back again tomorrow."

"Who says tomorrow?" Leric hefted the sack. "We have enough money and food to last us till we're far south. Why wait? We'll be on our way, with a good head start before the weather changes. Stow your things. We break camp at first light."

"So soon?" Rizka's heart clenched. "I thought I'd have time—"

"I'll get my things, too." Sofiya, with Petzel in her arms, had popped from behind Rizka's wagon. "I'll leave a note. It won't take me long."

Rizka snatched one of Sofiya's pigtails before the girl could dash off. "What things? What note?"

"So my parents will know. I'm going with you. We decided on it. You said I could."

"Little one, I never told you that."

"Yes, you did. Well—you never told me I couldn't."

"I'm telling you now." Rizka dislodged Petzel from Sofiya's arms. "You can't. You just plain can't. Not possible."

"Why?" blurted Sofiya. "I brought everybody here, didn't I? My idea, wasn't it? Go without me? No. That's not fair."

"Fair's got nothing to do with it. Listen to me," Rizka said, as Sofiya's lower lip began drooping to her chin. "You have your friends here, your family, everything you know."

"I don't care," Sofiya retorted. "I don't want a family. Why should I? You don't have one."

"Yes, I do." Rizka glanced at Leric and the *kumpania*, then turned her eyes on the empty clearing. For a moment, it filled again with voices and laughter; one by one, faces long familiar seemed to pass in front of her. "More than I thought.

"Mellish said they'd all come for my sake." She went to Big Franko, silently watching her. "Mellish"—she smiled at the recollection—"I remember him blowing kisses from his balloon. Letta crowning Pugash with a bucket. Esperanza and Lorins—they want me to be a godmother. And the time Fibich—Chief Councilor Fibich now—fell into a mudhole in Ali Baba's cave. And Karpath dancing that hornpipe on his boat.

"I never said good-bye to them." Rizka shook her head. After a moment, she added, "But it doesn't matter."

Big Franko looked at her, puzzled. "They were your friends; you were fond of them. It's not like you to say that."

"It doesn't matter," answered Rizka, "because—why should I say good-bye when I'm not leaving?"

"Your little finger!" Sofiya cried. "Your little finger told you to stay!"

"You listen to a finger?" Leric rubbed his ears as if they had conspired to trick him. "Practically a *rom* and you'll stay with *gorgios*? Crazy people! Full-blown fools!"

"Yes—but they're mine," Rizka said. "Besides, who's to keep them from making bigger fools of themselves? When Hatvan promotes himself to field marshal, suppose he tries to court-martial everybody, hup, hup? What if I'm gone and Pugash takes up doctoring again? And Sharpnack? You can be sure he won't stay a rat-catcher very long. He'll wiggle his way back. I'll have to be here to deal with him."

"That's true," Big Franko put in. "She has better sense than any of us. We can't do without Rizka. The townsfolk need her."

"And I need them," said Rizka. "One, especially."

"I loved my father," she went on. "I guess you can love someone you never really knew. I waited for him to come to me. I didn't have to. My truest father?" She put her arms around Big Franko. "He was here all the time."

"I waited, too," said Big Franko. "*Chiriklo*, welcome home."

Lloyd Alexander is the acclaimed author of more than thirty books for young people. His many honors include a Newbery Medal for *The High King*, a Newbery Honor for *The Black Cauldron*—both in the Prydain Chronicles—and National Book Awards for *The Marvelous Misadventures of Sebastian* and *Westmark*.

Lloyd Alexander lives with his wife, Janine, and their cats in Drexel Hill, Pennyslvania.